I0779199

THE DEAD FISH

Rajkamal Choudhary (1929–67) was an Indian poet, short story writer, novelist, critic and thinker. He wrote in both Maithili and Hindi and was well-versed in Bengali, having translated Shankar's *Chourangi* and Bani Ray's *Chokhe Amar Trishna* into Hindi. Choudhary was known as 'a bold leader of new poetry' for his experimental style. He was born Manindra Narayan Choudhary in Mahishi, Bihar, and people affectionately called him Phool Babu.

In his short lifespan of less than 38 years, he contributed more than one hundred short stories, several novels and plays, dozens of articles and essays, and hundreds of poems. Choudhary emerged as a monumental writer in his mother tongue, Maithili, as well as in Hindi.

He was one of the most iconic literary figures of his time, a trailblazer, a trendsetter and a visionary whose works resonate even today.

Mahua Sen is an author, poet and translator. A recipient of the Reuel International Poetry Prize, the Poesis Award for Excellence in Literature, and the Poet of the Year (2022) award by Ukiyoto Publishing, her recent book *Nostalgia Crafting a Home Within* (Red River)—an Amazon bestseller in Asian Literature—garnered the prestigious Maharshi Ved Vyas International Award for Poetry in 2024. The book was also shortlisted for the Banaras Lit Fest Book Awards.

For Mahua, writing is synonymous with breathing, and literature serves as a compass, guiding her through the promenade of existence. In the echoes of literature, she finds her voice.

Mahua is a management professional and lives in Hyderabad with her family. She can be reached at sen.mahua5@gmail.com.

'*The Dead Fish*, Mahua Sen's translation of Rajkamal Choudhary's daring novel *Machhali Mari Hui*, not only evokes the milieu of mid-20th-century Calcutta but also invades the space of current discussions on sexuality, social hierarchy and systemic corruption. The act of transferring the metaphoric language of the original into modern English is remarkably successful, as well as the time shifts that the author has played with. Like Choudhary, Sen retains a neutral tone in the sensitive portrayal of same-sex love and financial exploitation. With finesse, the translator uses a calibrated vocabulary to paint shades of meaning and catch the idioms. Sen's first-ever translation of this controversial Hindi novel is laudable for its accomplished narrative, and also for setting a new direction for gender studies.'

—Malashri Lal
Author, Critic and
Former Professor of English, University of Delhi

'Howsoever famous a writer may be in the public sphere of their own mother tongue, they enter the city space of a new linguistic culture almost like an orphan. This orphan, like any dazed child, walks quietly behind the translation artist who plays the godmother at every step. From the selection of the text to its publication and reception in the new language, the translation artist plays many delicate roles, and some bilingual scholars like Mahua Sen play it exceptionally well. The success of Mahua's translation lies in finding a middle way between a tiresomely faithful and beautiful rendition of the text. She is friends with the text, responsible and sensitive to the core. Like an efficient stage director, she creates a luminous bond between words, and her control of diction is unlike the control of an autocrat. She is fairly democratic and playful at the same time. Those who have read Rajkamal in the original will appreciate this.'

—Anamika
Poet, Social Worker, Novelist

THE DEAD FISH

RAJKAMAL CHOUDHARY
TRANSLATED BY MAHUA SEN

RUPA

Published by
Rupa Publications India Pvt. Ltd 2025
7/16, Ansari Road, Daryaganj
New Delhi 110002

Sales centres:
Bengaluru Chennai Hyderabad
Jaipur Kathmandu Kolkata
Mumbai Prayagraj

P-ISBN: 978-93-6156-820-6
E-ISBN: 978-93-6156-193-1

First impression 2025

10 9 8 7 6 5 4 3 2 1

Printed in India

For my dear friend
Sri Revatiraman Jha
you loved one of my old writings,
Ek Hi Vritt Ki Rekhayein *or* Lines of a Single Circle
with love…

'It rained. Water flooded...
the dried-up river.
The dead blue fish,
came back to life...'

Rajkamal Choudhary is an iconic figure in the Indian literary milieu of the 1960s. The Hungry Generation, to which he belongs, represents disillusionment, rebellion and a delirious wish to demolish all institutions crippling the freedom of an individual. The Hungryalists were rebels in every sphere of life, rejecting the reigning political, social and moral values, and celebrating life in its primitive purity, shorn of all external trappings.

The Hungry Generation was an all-India literary movement, though active mainly across the Bengali, Hindi and Telugu languages, and had close correspondence with the Beat Generation. They challenged conventional sexual mores, and their works often displayed outrageous attitudes towards sex and the institution of marriage. Even in their personal life, they were anti-establishment and somewhat bohemian. Their poetry was always offbeat, crafting an asymmetrical and disjointed crustacean structure, something radically new in Indian poetry. Rajkamal Choudhary's fiction as well as his poetry embodies most of these features. *Machhali Mari Hui* possibly registers them at their sharpest.

The narrative engages with upper-class life, not a very common thing at the time, exposing its rot, decadence and perversions. It is at times quite explicit in its treatment of sexual practices, where a decision regarding one's sexual orientation itself becomes a liberating force. This novel is remarkable for its form as well. This is the first Hindi novel, perhaps, that has a rambling form, making ample use of allusions and quotations and often lapsing into critical discourses. Despite all corporate intrigues and rottenness, life asserts itself and liberation comes through absolute renunciation.

Translated into English for the first time by Mahua Sen, a poet in her own right, *The Dead Fish* approximates the original Hindi text in every department. It must have been really difficult to carry over the feverish pitch of the Hindi syntax into English, but Mahua has done it exceedingly well, re-architecting the text for English readers. It is an eminently readable translation, faithful and flawless. This translation is worthy of appreciation, also for the reason that Mahua has picked up a text that's deviant in every way and subversive too, an enterprise rarely undertaken.

—Arun Kamal
Hindi Poet and Critic

Translator's Note

When a poet of the calibre of Rajkamal Choudhary turns his attention to prose, it's natural that the timbre and tone of the text will be extraordinary. Like his poetry, his fiction too is layered, lyrical, multifarious, rich in imagery and eloquent in symbolism, retaining the same poetic sensibility.

Machhali Mari Hui or *The Dead Fish* is not only a novel in the traditional sense of the term; rather, it is a work of profound narrative depth, exploring an artistic innovation in storytelling by preserving Choudhary's idiosyncratic poetic metronome throughout the story. This is a novel that only Rajkamal Choudhary could have written, and my humble attempt at translating it has been one of the most challenging yet rewarding experiences of my literary journey.

At its core, *The Dead Fish* is one of the finest portrayals of the post-independence Indian society, a time when the personal, in terms of choices, began to break free from the collective and the traditionally established narratives. It paints an era of cultural renaissance and reclaiming individual agency. The novel highlights this pendulum of transition with rare refinement. The author effortlessly delves into the intricacies of the dichotomy of personal desires and societal expectations, exploring human behaviour—the moral, emotional and psychological upheavals, when individuals assert their autonomy in terms of sexuality, aspirations, personal freedom and moral compass.

The most distinguished aspect of Rajkamal Choudhary's narrative style is the rustic undertone, embroidered with a fine filigree of a sophisticated and layered fabric with striking double entendre throughout the text. He aesthetically navigates between first- and third-person perspectives, creating a unique narrative voice that renders the readers multiple vantage points to view the story from. This writing style blurs the linearity of time, as it shifts back and forth, making the past and the present more fluid, sometimes even dimming the line between reality and imagination. This aspect of his style questions the traditional form of storytelling. It symbolizes the fractured and often muddled mayhem of human psychology and consciousness, delving deeper with a sincere exploration of inner lives, especially contexts that challenge social taboos.

Whether it is sexuality, gender roles or ethical dilemmas of the characters, *Machhali Mari Hui's* treatment of homosexuality, in particular, is handled with sensitivity, neutrality and empathy that was both rare and revolutionary for its time.

Choudhary's female characters, in particular, are given remarkable depth. They are neither idealized nor demonized, but presented with all their authentic human complexities. My goal in translating this work was to retain this sense of neutrality, to allow Choudhary's voice to speak without distortion or oversimplification. I wanted the English readers to encounter the same ambiguity, emotional intricacy and cultural richness that Hindi readers have long admired in his work.

The title itself, *The Dead Fish,* is a powerful metaphor that recurs throughout the novel. It stands for loss, decay, emotional stagnation and the slow withering of vitality, both in relationships and in the human spirit. The dead fish becomes a symbol of alienation, unfulfilled longing, and existential inertia, anchoring the novel's deeper philosophical concerns. Choudhary's mastery lies in how he weaves such symbols subtly into the narrative, allowing them to speak volumes without overt explanation. The way he blends the tactile physical world with a profound emotional truth creates a haunting and poignant atmosphere. Yet, despite these intricacies, Choudhary's art in keeping the readers soundly tethered to the emotional pulse of the story till the end is not only praiseworthy but rare.

This is a novel that deserves a wider, global readership. It is timeless in its concerns, bold in its treatment and profound in its psychological insights. Translating the work of Rajkamal Choudhary has not only been a fulfilling journey but also a learning lesson for me. I have tried to retain the original poetic quality and narrative shifts with utmost care and reverence, while rendering it into English that feels more accessible. I have also tried to preserve the cultural nuances, emotional depths and symbolic shades of the original text, aspiring to ensure that the English readers thoroughly experience Rajkamal Choudhary's thematic and stylistic intricacy, the courage of his voice and his unparalleled literary prowess.

—**Mahua Sen**
26.05.2025

Author's Note

In the year 1962 (June–July), two women from a friend's family were taken to the hospital together on account of mental health issues. ... I was writing this at that time. We would endlessly dawdle along the lanes of Moor Avenue to Free School Street in Calcutta like vagabonds and believed in the unbelievable, imaginary and indolent. ... Lalit Sharma, Uma Sehgal, Parmesh, Suryadev Singh Amar, Manju Haldar, Abhay Jain, Madanlal Sethi, Manav Gupta, Om Prakash Manchanda, Champa Kulshreshtha, Arundhati Mukherjee, Baiju Shah—we would meet at some crossroads, only to veer off into different lanes. To extend my gratitude towards them is neither appropriate nor required. ... Nor is it essential to mention that no individual's image, character or identity exists in *The Dead Fish*. This novel is born out of chance and coincidence, not from wishful experience. ... 'Kalyani Mansion' does not exist anywhere in Calcutta.

—Rajkamal Choudhary
'Kamayani'
Saidpur-Bhikhna Pahari
Patna-800004

Preface

One

Lesbians—meaning women engaging in same-sex love—have not been written about much, especially in Hindi novels. We do not get the chance to intimately witness the private lives and inner characters of Indian women. Sometimes, because of what is hidden, at other times, due to what is laid bare in front of our eyes.

Two

In 1959 (August), one of my short stories, 'The Sun with Twelve Eyes', was published in Ajmer's *Leher* magazine's special issue on short stories. I wrote another story, 'Oceanic', for the annual edition of *Vinod* (1961). I had to gather information and incidents regarding homosexuality for these two stories. ... However, while writing *The Dead Fish*, I realized I could use these incidents and information while narrating the story of Nirmal Padmavat.

Even in foreign languages, only a handful of books have been written on this subject. *Female Sex Perversion* by Dr Maurice Chideckel was published in 1935, and *Sex Variants* by George W. Henry, M.D., in 1941. Lesbianism was first talked about in these two books, and this kind of sexual activity was 'accepted' as a mental disorder.

In 1951, *The Homosexual in America* by Donald Webster

Cory and, in 1953, *The Second Sex* by Simone de Beauvoir were published. Thereafter, in 1954, a complete book on this subject, *Female Homosexuality* by Frank S. Caprio, was published. Besides these books, Dr Alfred C. Kinsey's book, *Sexual Behavior in the Human Female*, was published. There are also a few novels, stories and memoirs in the English literature. Diana Frederics' memoir was published in 1939 and caught the attention of intellectuals and psychologists from all over the world.

It seems unnecessary to mention that I have read all these books.

Three

Male homosexuality is illegal in almost all 'civilized' countries in the world. Women still have freedom in this regard in most countries. In cities like Paris, New York and Tokyo, affluent and independent women have created such clubs and rest houses where they indulge in various homosexual activities with their respective partners. Law is no impediment to this.

Renowned American judge Morris Ploscowe has raised this question in his book *Sex and the Law*. He questions why women have the freedom of such spontaneity that is forbidden for men.

Ploscowe and other conservative scholars and experts neither have the sensitivity nor liberality towards people with such sexual orientation. Regardless, these women demand the exertion of their own autonomy regarding desired (to the extent of 'perversion') sexual activity...

Four

There are no clubs for women in our country, nor do our women know how to conduct such things in a modern way.

In our country, despite indulging in homosexual

activities, most women do not realize what they are doing, nor the meaning of such activities… They certainly do it, but they do it in their slumber, inebriated, unknowingly. And gripped by superstition and ignorance, they continue to be too religious and too intimidated.

Five

After the last World War, a group of contemporary businessmen in Calcutta awoke one fine day with a revelation. They opened the closed coffers of capital, influence and industry to start new businesses in areas like Chowringhee, Dalhousie Square, Mahatma Gandhi Road, Dharmatala and Clive Street, where they sat in high-rise offices built in the American style.

Nirmal Padmavat is a businessman of this tribe. Despite owning such capital and the massive 'Kalyani Mansion', why did Nirmal turn rigid as a statue? That is not what my humble novel is about. It is not even about whether Shirin Padmavat had the right to live as the ordinary wife of an ordinary man. This novel is not about anything—it just hints at something.

—Rajkamal Choudhary
20.07.1965

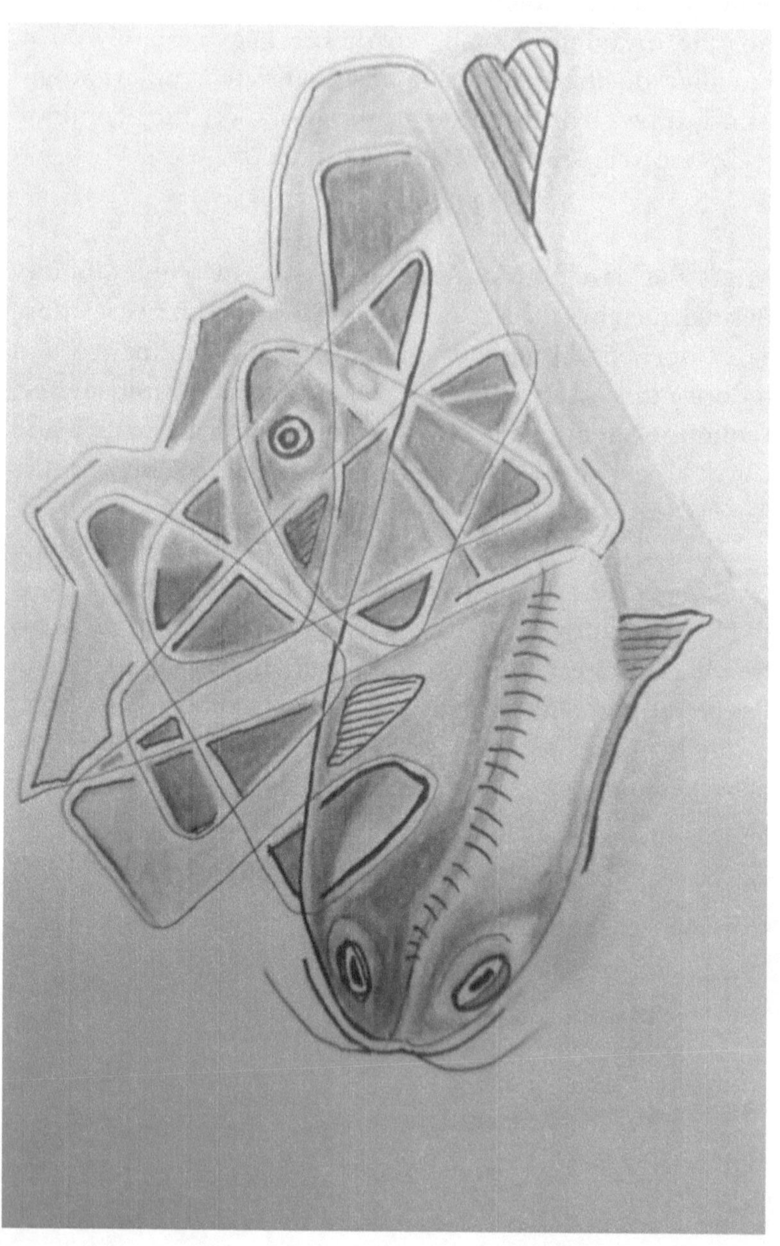

One

Who might have come at this odd hour? Who might this person be? What kind of a mask is he wearing? What are his intentions?

The doorbell continued to ring. The bell is not ringing—Dr Raghuvansh tried to convince himself. He told himself that the doorbell was not ringing and that there was no stranger waiting behind the door on the stairs. However, the illusion proved difficult to dispel. The noise was loud, disrupting his concentration. He found it increasingly challenging to focus. He felt light scattering in all directions, almost as if emanating from a cracked bulb. His ears began to ache as the noise broke his reverie.

As Priya went to unlatch the door, her father said, 'If it's not an urgent medical case, ask them to come in the morning.'

Dr Raghuvansh is an eminent surgeon and is equally noble. Nobody has such medical prowess as he at Sheetaldas Medical College. There is no one else in his family, only his daughter Priya, who is eighteen. She studies at the same medical college in the third year. She is intelligent, obedient, brimming with confidence. She has inherited her mother's intrinsic nature. Her father has never felt the need to discipline her; rather, he believes in natural growth and evolution. He doesn't preach, unlike ordinary Indian fathers, that the stole should not hang around her neck like a serpent, the shirt should be buttoned up, and so on.

Priya does not require such advice because she is smart. She is not inclined towards hanging out with college boys. She stays aloof, reticent and unapproachable to others. Even though Priya has inherited her mother's temperament, her personality is more like her father's.

Priya suddenly started to yell. Such screams in their sleep are not uncommon among women gripped by insane delusions. Progressing from the door, echoing through the porch, rebounding off the walls and seemingly causing injuries, her protracted and mournful scream gradually diminished in Dr Raghuvansh's private room. The table lamp's light was dimmed, and Kalyani, depicted in a life-size oil painting on the front wall, appeared to cease smiling. Dr Raghuvansh lifted his head, directing his gaze towards the door.

He was engrossed in the *British Medical Journal*. An important essay on the potentialities of cancer treatment has been published. The writer, Dr Romanoff, was associated with him for quite a few months at New York's National Research Institute. But Priya's scream was still lingering in his room. Securing his glasses, he got up from his chair and asked, 'What happened, Pri? What's wrong?'

Pri came panting, almost fainting, and hugged her father's sturdy frame. What she had seen was something akin to a royal Bengal tiger spanning twelve yards, standing at the top of the stairs near the door. It resembled a Black genie emerging out of Alladin's lamp. *Your wish is my command, Alladin. What do you fancy? Princess of Persia? Devadasi of Kamarupa? Egypt's…!* In a manner reminiscent of a character from Chinese folk tales, an individual clad in a black cloak, wielding a black magic wand and a black handkerchief adorning their head, materialized at the door. Raghuvansh became concerned upon seeing his daughter in such a vulnerable condition. He wondered, *what type of sound could cause this fearless girl of Kalyani to faint.* Caressing Priya's hair and back and, mentally chanting the name of his deity, he said, 'Come back to your senses! Look here, Pri, what am I asking? Look here...'

Priya clung tightly to Dr Raghuvansh's chest, her arms wrapped around him in a firm embrace, but she was quivering like the flame of a diya in a strong wind. After a while, she spoke somewhat tearily, 'Papaji, the light bulb at the door has exploded. A Black man is standing in the dark, like a genie. His eyes are gleaming like a torch and Papaji, he is holding a rifle in his hands... Perhaps he is not a Black man but a genie...'

He needs a walking stick to support his left leg. Nirmal Padmavat, the owner of 'Kalyani Mansion', refrains from venturing outside without his walking stick, which is made from black walnut. Not a rifle, but he always holds the stick in his left hand.

Dr Raghuvansh started laughing, and his mirth seemed to brighten up the entire apartment. The light in the room became more radiant. Nirmal had already entered and was standing inside the room. Priya, initially embarrassed, quickly regained her composure. *This man is not a ghost but a human being.* However, after a moment, Priya felt enraged as soon as Nirmal uttered, 'Doctor, Baby was scared to see me.'

Why is this man calling me 'baby'? On what basis? Priya felt small in the presence of this unfamiliar man. It was as if she had transformed into a tiny Japanese doll, intimidated, embarrassed and after a moment, indignant. The sight of Nirmal on the stairs itself had turned her into a doll, leaving her stupefied and bewildered. Her heart skipped a beat when she realized that before her stood an imposing, seven-feet-eight-inch tall, man.

And his eyes glittered like large, shapeless pieces of sapphire. Holding a bare rifle, his face angry, he exuded a primitive aura. It was as if this man was about to point the barrel of his rifle between Priya's legs. As if, shredded into pieces by the .303 bullets, lumps of her flesh and droplets of her blood would spread at her own doorstep. Priya ran to her father's room, howling, for safety.

Walking slowly and wearing a small smile, Nirmal followed Priya to Dr Raghuvansh's room. Priya was on the verge of leaving the room when her father made the introductions. 'Nirmal, this is my daughter, Priya. She takes after her mother in everything. And listen Pri, Nirmal has come here for the first time. Nirmal Padmavat! I had to visit Vienna last month just for his sake; you already know him.'

Sheetaldas Hospital could open its new neurosurgical department only because of Nirmal Padmavat's generous donation of twenty-five lakh rupees. The towering thirty-storied building, Kalyani Mansion, located on Princess Street, is still the tallest in Calcutta. The loftiest. No one could have imagined such a tall and wide skyscraper in our country. Nirmal realized his dreams and, in turn, provided accommodation to fifteen hundred middle-class families.

Around the same time, Nirmal Padmavat began to face censure as well as praise in the city's social circles. A girl from Kalyani Mansion says, 'Nirmal Babu practices occult, he possesses knowledge of witchcraft. Those who defy him, death comes to them.' Countless rumours of this nature have circulated: Nirmal Babu is a criminal. He has amassed a lot of money, a lot of wealth, a huge estate, through nefarious deeds. Nirmal Babu makes the rogue employees of his office and the young women picked up from the upscale areas of the city stand in a row, strips them naked, and thrashes them with a whip. The rogue employees cannot even complain. Oftentimes, women faint even before being beaten up naked… They die.

Priya lacked the courage to utter a simple 'how do you do'. She could not even muster enough courage to lift her puffy eyelids and smile. She stood there under the secure shadow of her father. Then, unexpectedly, she spoke with a sprightly tone, infused with a mysterious reassurance, 'Why don't both of you sit and relax? I'll check if I can fetch some tea or coffee. Mahari has gone off to sleep...'

Nirmal smiled, pulled out a chair and settled down. He discerned that Priya was finding it challenging to endure his sharp and stern gaze. She seemed eager to run away and free herself from his scrutiny. *Will you be able to escape, Priya? Can this girl summon the strength to flee—much like Kalyani?* Nirmal contemplated this. He understands people's minds effortlessly.

Understanding people doesn't demand effort from him; rather, he possesses an innate talent for it. His ability extends beyond comprehending just the mind; in the blink of an eye, he can perform a circumambulation of the entire existence of the person before him. This is what he has done all his life. He doesn't need to do or attain anything more than this.

Pritam Singh's eyes are fixed on the windshield, but he is contemplating his decision. He resolves that he will no longer take his wife on outings in his employer's imposing Chevrolet, even if the owner is out of town. Mrs Chakravarty is playing table tennis at the club and wants to sell all her shares in Western Tube Company to Nirmal Padmavat at the highest price. Nirmal tells her, 'I don't play tennis, missus, not even on the table. *You* may like table tennis, I don't!'

Seth Bilvamangal Das will burst into peals of laughter, will get up from his chair and advance straight to the bathroom, one of whose doors open into the mansion. He will query his ailing wife stationed at the door, and she will affirm with a 'yes'. Nirmal is aware that the prosperous merchant's wife won't refuse, given their acquaintance.

Nirmal's eyes resemble two fully opened seashells, exuding a radiance akin to black pearls. Priya cannot tolerate these pearls. Yet, the radiance extends beyond his eyes; Nirmal's personality is darker than ebony itself. His body bears the weight of hundreds of thick layers of China ink, leaving only his eyes, which are white!

Within these eyes, Padmavat's intelligence, honesty, simplicity, nobility and crookedness co-exist—the softness of butter and hardness of stone, everything resides. Everything is crystal clear. Visible, and yet elusive. They serve as both a transparent mirror as well as a thick wall of steel. That's why those who know him from afar respect him, despise him and fear him all at once. Some people have read Alexandre Dumas' famous novel *The Count of Monte Cristo*, others have heard the stories of Arthur, the black-robed prince of Britain, while some have this habit of exaggerating the truth, stretching its dimensions to observe, listen and recount it.

'I'll go get coffee,' Priya told her father, stole a glance at Nirmal and went out the door. Dr Raghuvansh started smiling. Padmavat said, 'It isn't right to visit so late in the night without any prior intimation.'

'I sensed you would come today,' Doctor responded in clear tones. It was not necessary to say that eleven years ago on this very day, Nirmal Padmavat had set foot in Calcutta for the first time. Calcutta, which was deemed the quirkiest and most peculiar city in Asia. On that day, Padmavat himself was a stranger in the city, an outsider adrift in his own peculiarity.

Who was he? What did he want in this city and from whom? Who had invited him here?

Dr Raghuvansh was returning home after burying Priya's mother at the Park Street Cemetery. Little Priya, barely six or seven years old, accompanied him. However, she was not crying for her mother; instead, she was fretful about getting an ice cream from Kwality Ice Cream Parlour. It started raining, a common occurrence in the capricious climate of Calcutta, where randomness seems to extend its wings to everything.

Doctor had a white handkerchief in his hand, which had a flower embroidered on one of its corners with delicate silken thread. Priya continued to become restless for an ice cream.

The evening crowd and vehicles were piling up in Park Street. A White lady paused briefly to exchange greetings with the Doctor before continuing on her way. Perched on a hand-pulled rickshaw, the lady seemed to be going to a hotel on Ganesh Chandra Avenue—a routine she followed every evening. Dr Raghuvansh smiled—each of his patients recognized this typical smile of his. His ageing countenance expressed a sweet, generous and somewhat forlorn smile that never stretched too wide or felt overly poignant.

Dr Raghuvansh stood for several minutes, holding Priya's hand, on the patio of Kwality. It was common knowledge that the Doctor's wife had passed away earlier that morning, but none of the acquaintances or strangers passing by extended words of sympathy or comfort. A momentary pause, a sentence or even just a nod of social etiquette, thereafter, people continued on their way to their restaurant, hotel or business, cracking jokes, sharing smiles, following the established rhythm of an evening on Park Street.

Japanese tourist Tako Yushikura has written in his travel memoirs (1950), that despite being so small, there is no other city in the world that has such a magnificent street. Park Street is a little street—it begins at the life-size bronze statue of Gandhiji in Chowringhee, meandering through Free School Street and Lower Circular Road, and ends there. The new building of the Asiatic Society; a row of motorcar company showrooms; the modern painting association Artistry House hidden in one corner; Peiping, a Chinese restaurant; Trincas, another restaurant, followed by Kwality restaurant; English magazines are scattered on porches, featuring on their covers half-naked young women; Mrs Fatakdawala peacefully dozes on the Dunlopillo mattress of 'India Hair Cutting and Dressing Salon'. Mr Kapoor is a regular at the Olympia Bar and stays till 11 p.m. 'Kalyani Mansion' remains aglow all night, illuminated by red, blue and white lights, casting a dim flame over the country's largest apartment house.

It is said that night starts after midnight at Park Street when people from Dalhousie Square, Chowringhee and nearby small and big streets and hotels venture out in their own and their friends' small and large cars, attempting to discreetly enter one of the houses or flats on Park Street, shrouded in darkness and bathed in the soft glow of blue lights. There is silence around St Xavier's College, and rickshaw pullers, clutching a bell in their fingers, create a *ting-ting, ding-ding* sound, signalling to pedestrians passing by.

The signal, once clear, never loses its clarity. Everyone understands. Nights at Park Street begin four hours before dawn and conclude four hours after. A jobseeker, Miss Lovleena Dasgupta, asks her roommate in their rental, Miss Rodrigues, for a cigarette, 'Can you give me a Charminar?' Miss Rodrigues, stretching in her bed, emerges from under the mosquito net and shares an incident with her friend. 'After you dozed off, your friend started talking to me for a very long time. But I told him, "Your friend has fallen asleep. You must leave now."' At 9 a.m., both friends, sipping tea and smoking cigarettes, recite their morning prayers.

Prayers that are still prayers and have not devolved into grievances or abuses. Though prayers are uttered, the morning lacks its usual serenity, and the atmosphere is devoid of the right conditions for such sacred offerings. At the time of Kalyani's death, Dr Raghuvansh too had offered similar prayers, yet the dissonant climate seemed to deny the fulfilment of his plea. Not even earlier today at the Park Street Cemetery. Nobody listens to the Doctor. He is always inundated with futile offers—rewards and possibilities that hold no value for him. What use is the support of this young girl when compared to the absence of Kalyani? This is not the prayer he had sought.

The rain ceased, and Priya began to insist on getting an ice cream. *It doesn't matter that her mother is not there. She will get an ice cream.* He entrusted Priya to the care of a nurse seated in his car parked on the sidewalk of Mounolia. He said to the nurse, 'Treat her to some ice cream and then take her home. I don't need the car; I'll come home late.'

Even at that age, she could sense her father's anger, boredom and irritation. Without uttering a word, Priya looked on with unwavering attention as he navigated the road, exercising caution around the vehicles.

Having been immersed in love for two decades, if the spell suddenly shatters, why wouldn't one find solace in a bottle of Scotch? Why wouldn't you contemplate breaking the bottle on your head? Confronted by an overwhelming sense of helplessness and the presence of an unseen force, wouldn't the urge arise to inflict self-harm? Yet, not in the manner of Shirin–Farhad from Parsi theatre, but more like Ramakrishna Paramhansa, the enigma of death must first be unravelled…

Pulling over her boat at the ghat of the Hooghly, a woman resembling a princess stepped into the courtyard of the Dakshineswar temple. Paramhansa, sitting in Panchvati, his prayer grove, was observing her. The princess, strolling gracefully, with a bowed head and a warm smile, was walking towards him. Paramhansa discerned her pregnancy as she drew nearer, her belly visibly swelled. Eventually, at a distance from him, she gave birth to a baby. She cradled the newborn in her arms and gently reclined on the floor. Paramhansa saw with his own eyes that the mysterious princess, sitting right there on the edge of Panchavati, cut her child into pieces and devoured every part of him, his bones, flesh, blood, hands, feet, head. After this, she rose and returned to the Hooghly.

Ramakrishna Paramhansa had gained a profound understanding of the essential enigma of death. Kalyani shared this story with the Doctor, explaining, 'There is minimal distinction between death and birth, neither of location nor of time. The disparity, rather, resides in life itself. It's akin to King Janaka's sword suspended by a delicate thread between birth and death, and we, in turn, slumber beneath this sword in fear.'

Dr Raghuvansh confidently walked into an English bar. Whenever he drinks alcohol, he prefers Scotch. After the third or fifth or eighth peg, oblivious to the number, a man came and stood near his table. Doctor did not even look at him for a few minutes, as he was engrossed in Kalyani's words and thoughts. She used to apprise him of uncanny incidents and stories. If one listened without probing for truth or falsehood, one would agree that she had a knack for spinning captivating stories about death, love, and gods and goddesses.

But if someone comes and stands beside the table, acknowledging their presence becomes unavoidable. The bar was relatively empty due to the rain. Waiters were engaged in conversation near the door. At a distance in the corner, an old man wept, hunched over a glass of beer, like a broken branch of hawthorn. Two boys in jeans and silk t-shirts were drinking Coca-Cola from blue glasses, or perhaps, 3X rum! An Anglo-Indian girl was talking to the bar manager and was chuckling, pointing towards Dr Raghuvansh's table.

Doctor would have been offended but the man began to smile, and his black irises sparkled with the sweetness of empathy. He didn't remain a stranger anymore. He stated in a clear and beautiful accent, 'Doctor Raghuvansh!' Saying this, he perched on a chair in front of Raghuvansh. He did not need to ask for permission to sit. He took the Doctor's right palm that was on the table in both his hands and said, 'Do not insult death... This Scotch disrespects Kalyani.'

The mention of Kalyani's name from Nirmal Padmavat left Dr Raghuvansh reeling, and his face drained of colour.

Nirmal looked like the prince of some mythical demon country, possessing a melodic voice akin to Black singers, and features sculpted from black stone like that of the Greek gods. *Why does this man talk about death and memory and their humiliation like Rilke and Rimbaud? Who is this man?* The doctor inquired, 'Who are you?'

'Two years ago, a picture of you was published in the *Times* in connection with a brain operation. I was in New York at the time. I know you from there. I arrived in Calcutta this morning, in fact just a short while ago, and read about Mrs Raghuvansh's unfortunate passing and her obituary in the evening newspapers. I spotted you at the table as I entered here.' Nirmal said these things in a direct manner and a subdued tone before signalling the bartender.

Dr Raghuvansh did not ask any questions regarding his identity after this, not even his name. They sat quietly. Nirmal ordered a full bottle of Old Smuggler and kept the doctor company. The woman at the counter asked the good doctor via a message sent through the waiter, 'May I meet you?' When Nirmal refused by gesturing with his hand, the woman got scared. She picked up her bag from the counter and darted out of the bar.

Dr Raghuvansh could not recollect anything about his wife. The presence of this man suddenly erased all his misery and distress. He felt as if there was no Kalyani, not even Priya. He could only feel the presence of this man who was smiling and sitting opposite him like a black rock cliff. Dr Raghuvansh was silent and he seemed intoxicated.

Brain operation…neurosurgery…cancer…haemorrhage… nurses resembling phantom shadows in their white attire… operation theatre…the floodlight above the head…the semi-conscious woman on the operating table, moaning in mild pain…moaning for what seemed like an eternity.

Blood pressure. Convulsion. Uraemia. Diabetes. Tumour. Brain tumour. Each word evokes a different picture, just like a picture in a black frame. 'No doctor, there is no brain tumour... The spine was punctured and examined—

the pressure is high, but the fluid is absolutely clear—the cerebrospinal fluid is normal... There are no cells, and the disc is also not jammed...it is flat... NPN and creatinine are also normal.'

'No Doctor, there's no brain tumour!'

'Then what is it? If it's not a brain tumour, then what is afflicting my wife? What has happened to her? Does this disease not have a name? Isn't there a cure?'

'Dr Raghuvansh! We cannot do anything but wait.'

Dr Raghuvansh could not do anything to save his wife. In the operation theatre of Sheetaldas Medical College Hospital, under the gleaming floodlights, Kalyani was lying unconscious. All famous surgeons and doctors of the city were gathered around her, praying, as if watching a spectacle. Staff nurse Malati Bai told the house surgeon Jatin Dasgupta, 'We haven't seen such a complex case in the past 10 years.' Dr Raghuvansh had telephoned Dr Bidhan Chandra Roy but unfortunately, he was in Delhi. Had Bidhan Roy been there, perhaps Mrs Raghuvansh would have recovered.

After Hakim Ajmal Khan, Bidhan Chandra Roy—the chief minister of West Bengal—was the most respected in the field of medical sciences. However, Bidhan Roy was not available at that point, and other doctors of the city struggled to detect this form of Kalyani's disease, with unfortunately no positive outcome. Priya's mother, holding her husband's hand, under the mournful and helpless gaze of doctors, drifted into her final slumber.

Priya's mother was buried at the cemetery, but Priya did not shed a tear since she could not comprehend that her mother was gone forever. When they began to place Kalyani in the coffin, Priya thought that she had just fallen asleep and they were placing her on the cot. A peaceful smile adorned the face of the lifeless body—a smile reminiscent of eyes immersed in slumber and lips drenched in love. It is often said that only the faces of ascetics remain unperturbed after death, but Kalyani had never embraced renunciation throughout her long and expansive life. Much like plants draw sustenance from the earth, she absorbed the essence of others into her own being. The yearning for this vital essence persisted within her, both internally and externally, and it never waned.

It was a thought to ponder upon as to why her face was shimmering with a blue aura even after death.

Priya was having her ice cream at Kwality. The nurse sitting beside her was contemplating about what her master, Dr Raghuvansh, would do now? Would he remarry? Or would he be swept up in a whirlwind romance with a nurse or a lady doctor? She was lost in these thoughts.

Meanwhile, Nirmal Padmavat was waiting silently for Dr Raghuvansh's answers at the bar. He had asked Doctor a question a moment ago, 'Did Kalyani give birth to a girl six years ago?'

He failed to mention to Nirmal that his daughter, Priya, was having ice cream in the nearby Kwality restaurant. He was startled to find that the man in front of him knew so much about him. He had yet to absorb this information. He was wondering why and how he knew so much. And despite knowing all this, why did he come to him only after Kalyani's death?

Death, once a profound mystery, no longer occupies the minds of French existentialists and Russian scientists. What is death?—nobody asks this question anymore. Everyone knows the answer. Death, God, chance, terror, religion, affection or anything of this 'pattern' is no longer a mystery or a secret. No saint or messiah of the contemporary era would have any objection in considering one's own talent as the I, that is, the 'will' as the supreme being. Individuals, each in their own unique way, define their personal God and love and even choose a specific date for their death. Swami Vivekananda had told one of his American disciples, 'New chapters will be added to the book of God; there will always be the origination of new truths and forms. I pray that hundreds of sects will emerge from one sect and a time will come when each person becomes a friend of his personal sect.'

Friend to his sect, and creator of his God!... 'Did Kalyani give birth to a girl, six years ago?'... Kalyani had created her own God in the form of Priya. It's not only about Priya, or Kalyani; every living being in the world, through their unique experience of death, contributes to the creation of something new. So, did Kalyani create Priya?

Three

While leaving the bar, Nirmal detained Dr Raghuvansh at the door and said three things: one, he came to this city just that day and now intends to stay there; two, neurosurgery has not seen much progress in our country and Kalyani fell prey to the complications of the surgery; and three, while he couldn't make promises due to financial constraints—currently lacking even a thousand or five thousand rupees—he would exert his utmost effort.

Parting ways with an aristocratic handshake and a superficial smile, Doctor felt Nirmal Padmavat's palms were robust and unusually hot, almost burning. Nirmal did not give him a chance to say anything. He said, 'I will visit you, Doctor.'

Raghuvansh was now in his senses. The alcohol had run through his veins, and he was starting to recognize this stranger a bit. He said, 'I shall wait. It's your home, you can come anytime.'

Nirmal called for a hand-pulled rickshaw and hopped onto it. Doctor went to Kwality to check on Priya, who was now happy and pacified. She likes the ambience of this place. She used to sit with her mother out there, in one of the corners. The jukebox played music, and Priya, now happy, asked Dr Raghuvansh, 'Papaji, can I play a song?'

As soon as she put money in the jukebox, an LP record

popped up, began to hum, then emerged at the surface and reverberated throughout the restaurant. The meaning of the first line of the English song was that city girls were unfaithful. If you asked them for a tobacco box, they would give you a red tomato! Dr Raghuvansh was engrossed in this song for a long time, and Priya continued asking her father the meaning of this song while gazing and giggling at the vibrant girls around her. The doctor began explaining the song's meaning to her.

Nirmal proceeded towards the Park Street Cemetery. *Even for a few moments, one must turn philosophical. She deserves at least this much,* he thought. As he stood by Kalyani's freshly dug grave, he silently conveyed, *I've arrived, Kalyani. I'm here with you…*

But he stopped at the green wooden gate made in an inverted V shape. There was no bouquet of white flowers in his hands. *He had not come to repeat any anecdote from New York or the French Riviera. Then why should he give flowers to Kalyani,* he defended himself. For a minute, he was tempted to stand near that grave, freshly made of concrete, while imagining Kalyani emerging from there in flesh and blood. He thought if that happened, he would say, 'Let's go for an all-night taxi ride tonight.' He would walk down Park Street lanes holding Kalyani's icy cold hand. But at this point, he collected his thoughts from meandering. Standing near the gate, he accepted the reality that Kalyani was gone and that he shouldn't disturb her eternal slumber.

Many flower vendors selling bouquets approached him and insisted that he buy them. 'I don't want to,' he said so sharply, innumerable times, that it terrified the boys. They thought that this dark-skinned sahib had lost his composure. 'I—do—not—want—to,' said Nirmal for the last time, and then swiftly left. A crowd gathered at the intersection of the

Free School Street, where a *been* was being played.

Nirmal was alien to such a congregation. Nirmal had read in one of the Bengali novels that there were three significant places to visit in Calcutta—the Pice Hotel and the settlements in Kholabadi and Kalighat. It dawned on him that he had not explored the city yet.

Tens of thousands of people have fallen asleep with their heads resting on the ticket windows of cinema halls. The dome of the Ochterlony Monument is adorned with thousands of gallows, resembling balance scales, from which dangle miniature houses, radiograms, whisky bottles and heaps of government files tethered by both small and large ropes. Thirteen thousand grocers broke their hands and arms after leaping off the roof of the Writers' Building. The massive garden across from the Calcutta High Court, the Eden Gardens—likened to the Garden of Eden where Adam first plucked the forbidden fruit—is now reflected in the stony pupils of ailing women. A procession of Shyambazar–Belgachia was started by the kings of a company of small children studying A–B–C–D–E–F. Now it has reached Jadavpur, Sonpur, Durgapur.

Hunger, cancer nestled between the hips, newspapers brimming with images of scantily clad girls, Kali Temple, fifty-three Kali temples, foreign tourists with their eyes fixed on their binoculars and cameras... Who is 'Lalbibi'?... What is *gulabchhadi*, my friend?…Youngsters auctioning desi fountain pens along every footpath of Dalhousie–Dharmatala–Chowringhee disappear with their 'merchandise' into the adjacent streets even before the *halla gadi* arrives. What is this 'halla gadi'? And what is the stock market?

Nirmal has no knowledge of the language and religion, lifestyle and history, fashion and rules and regulations of the people of this city. However, his purpose in coming here is to capture the pharaohs' wealth, the eighteen-year-old Queen Cleopatra and the Nile River.

The dominant force in this place is the stock market. Next to the market stand temples adorned with golden domes, juxtaposed with squalid slums and tall, imposing buildings that do not even allow fresh air or light to enter them. In this setting, women are the most vulnerable, whether leading the life of a sex worker or living the life of a traditional wife, being pregnant and again being pregnant, repeatedly; they inhabit a world foreign to him.

Kalyani was his only source of introduction to that life. Now she is no more. Nirmal stepped into the city, reached the Great Eastern Hotel suite, departed from Dum Dum airport, and Kalyani was gone. Why was she gone? Could it be that, lying half-conscious and somewhat deranged on the operation table, Kalyani somehow intercepted a telepathic signal? Did she possess an awareness of Nirmal's arrival?

It ought to be dismissed as mere coincidence because there is no means to find the reason and meaning behind these incidents. Not even during moments of leisure. But Nirmal doesn't believe in coincidences. He believes in being calculative; directing hatred towards the one you love most inevitably leads to a disarrayed mind, a surge in depression, a frail heart and an afflicted brain. It is almost a natural progression for death to follow. Kalyani died. Yet, being in close proximity to the deceased or lingering near her was an impossibility.

Nirmal had met a Bengali saint in California. That saint purportedly summoned departed souls to his table for sustenance and comfort. Nirmal befriended him and expressed his concern, asserting that such a practice was not only ethically questionable but also criminal. The saint replied, 'What is left that is not a crime? Democracy?

Commercial dominion? War? Whatever we do, we do by His command, that is, what we do, we do not actually do it, rather our Father, our God makes us do it.'

Nirmal concluded that in any significant city of the twentieth century, saints, ruling politicians and women renowned for their art of draping and undraping a sari would attain enlightenment and *moksha*. Visualizing these three figures, with devoted merchants following closely behind, hands folded, heads bowed and eyes closed, Nirmal envisioned a spiritual pursuit.

I will not become a part of the tribe of Galileo or Plato, Nirmal resolved after coming out of the office of the Bengali saint. He never changed his vow. Not even after visiting Dr Raghuvansh's house and seeing Priya.

'Doctor, I am not a part of the crowd, that's why I didn't visit you earlier. I was preoccupied and didn't have the time. Even now I do not have the time and my health is also not good. A stone crusher machine seems to persist in its relentless churning in my head. Had you not arrived in Vienna on time, the doctors of Pelberg Home would have killed me. They marvelled at the fact that I was conscious despite running a temperature of 105... Why didn't I start spouting my story in delirium? Even now the condition is the same. The machine continues its rumbling. But I'm glad I've come this far. To this waterfall, to this blue river that people consider love and dignity.'

Nirmal's tranquil and pleasant gaze told all these things to Dr Raghuvansh. The doctor listened. An old photograph of Kalyani hangs above the book rack. Nirmal's eyes twinkle. However, he remained reticent. He talks very little. Moreover, Doctor didn't even ask anything. He doesn't even prefer asking his patients too many questions. He just examines and diagnoses. Dr Raghuvansh, much like Nirmal, possesses a similar approach. He is not one to bombard his patients with numerous questions. Instead, he prefers examination and understanding. In their shared disposition, the Doctor appeared reminiscent of an aged, gaunt Greek philosopher, while Padmavat exuded the majesty and chivalry of a Roman warrior. Padmavat's nature, characterized by aggression and combat, found triumph in approaching battles with the surety of inevitable surrender. His initial strikes were not fuelled by the unstable emotions of anger, enthusiasm or bravery but by steadfast and unwavering determination.

Dr Raghuvansh asked, 'Did Mrs Sanyal meet you? Is the work over...?'

'I have notified the overseas bank that she will have access to the foreign exchange she requires in France,' Nirmal replied, bowing his head. Mrs Sanyal is an artist. She is travelling to Paris for her art exhibition. She needs a lot of funds there. She was a student of Dr Raghuvansh at Sheetaldas Medical College. She had transitioned into the realm of art after marrying a high-ranking official in the Home Ministry. Now she lives alone. Govind Ballabh Pant's home ministry sacked Mr Sanyal for accepting bribes. Mrs Sanyal took her jewellery and alimony, choosing to separate from her husband. No honest artist can live with a corrupt officer.

'She was troubling me a lot. I didn't have an alternative, that's why I sent her to you. She was my student...'

'She told me.'

'Have you seen her paintings? Does she paint great pictures, eh? Or is it more of a fashionable pursuit?'

'She had brought her paintings with her. But I didn't buy any paintings. There was no space in my room for paintings. I have done what she requested though.'

Dr Raghuvansh understood what his young friend was

saying and smiled. Padmavat began to light a cigarette. Priya came in with a nurse and kept the coffee on the table. She was trying to escape Nirmal's gaze. The nurse asked Doctor, 'Sir, you have to go to the hospital once. That brain tumour case...'

Mrs Sanyal visited Nirmal's flat at nine in the morning with eight to ten of her paintings. Nirmal had constructed a four-room flat on the roof of Kalyani Mansion, equipped with air conditioning and heat control. Access to the flat was restricted, permitted only for Dr Raghuvansh, *khansama* Ali, private secretary Dhanwantlal and Nirmal's Alsatian dogs.

Nirmal's flat housed a teleprinter of the Press Trust, a radiogram, large steel almirahs, a refrigerator, landlines and an assortment of small and large machines. In one corner stood a small weighing machine. The walls were adorned with a vast picture of the Himalayas, a creation by the painter Roerich, stretching from wall to wall. The bedroom contained a simple bed and featured a statue of Dakshina Kali on the wall, her red tongue lolling out, a *khadaga* in one of the left hands and a severed head in the other, with the remaining two right hands depicting *abhayamudra* and *varadamudra*.

This statue of Dakshina Kali, originating from a temple in Nepal's Terai region, found its way to Nirmal Padmavat's bedroom. Nirmal would sleep in the presence of this idol. He used to pandiculate in front of this idol after waking up from his slumber. And coming out of the room, he would leisurely stroll on the open terrace of the city's tallest building, observing the sleeping city below at two o'clock in the night. The Dakshina Kali in a frame hanging on the wall at times smiled and at other times transformed into a more grotesque, naked and darker representation, seemingly driven by bloodlust. Contemplating the fog-enveloped Victoria Memorial, Nirmal pondered the vast temporal and civilizational gaps between this monument and Kalyani Mansion—the Sun temple of Konark, the Buddhist caves of Ajanta, the Taj Mahal of Agra, the Ochterlony Monument, and this Kalyani Mansion. Nirmal desired to perceive and experience all these monuments as part of a single continuum, a unified definition. *Kalyani Mansion is a mausoleum.*

Every night at two o'clock, Nirmal Padmavat would rise from his bed and venture into the open terrace. There he wandered, observing the transformative hues of the marshy waters of the Hooghly illuminated by the brightness from dredgers and ships. The small dovecote-like windows of the new secretariat. The Howrah Bridge stretching out like a fishnet in the fog. A girl with big eyes smoking a cigarette in a neon sign advertising the cigarette manufacturers, Marcovitch & Co. Dakshineswar on this side, Belur Math on the other. Fields, and more fields. Small parks. Even smaller lanes. Lane after lane. Houses and endless houses. The oval dome of Mahajati Sadan. The golden peaks of Jain temples shimmering in the moonlit night, a testament to the enduring presence of religion and the unwavering flame of love within the depths of humanity.

Rashmoni, the queen of the fishermen and sailors, builds a temple for her deity. An old Englishman puts a marble slab on the grave of his dead wife, and writes on it 'I loved her, she was my wife'. The old man has not been able to build a tomb for his love. He just writes on a piece of stone 'I loved her'. In these acts of religious devotion and personal love, individuals inscribe their words onto tangible symbols, be it a temple or a gravestone, expressing that which gives meaning to their existence and a desire to endure beyond their mortal years.

Nirmal Padmavat stands atop the tombstones, thinking that there exists no distinction between Dakshina Kali and Kalyani. In his perception, both embody two facets of matriarchy, akin to the symmetry of two eyes or two bosoms. Having transcended duality, Nirmal returns to a state of non-duality and returns to his bedroom. Facing Dakshina Kali, he becomes immersed in the crimson gaze of Kalyani. In this immersion, he abandons the desire to resurface, like a solitary island forsaking its place in the vastness of the sea. However, the limitations of the physical body bind man. Until the opportune moment arrives, he remains unable to surpass the constraints of his corporeal existence, regardless of his inner strength.

Kalyani had ruptured the limitations. Nirmal is trying to mend them again.

Returning from the gate of the Park Street Cemetery, Nirmal went straight to his hotel. 'Get the flask, bring the coffee. And listen, I don't want anything else,' he said to the waiter in his room.

The waiter quickly grasped that the gentleman had arrived in Calcutta solely for business, showing little inclination for leisure. Such pragmatic travellers are not often favoured by hotel staff. The sahibs who come with a woman, other than their wives, the waiters of posh hotels consider him their 'good luck'. In the hotels, like those of the standard of Great Eastern, very few guests have the habit of staying with their wives. However, lone travellers mostly do not come to such hotels. The 'receptionist' of their office accompanies them. Or any modern-minded steno girl. 'Meet my secretary, she is my inspiration. My "touch-me-sweet-girl",' the owner of one company, sitting on Eastern's large overhanging balcony, floating in the 'Old Smuggler's' boat, says to the owner of another company.

After a while, both the owners, while holding onto the waist of their secretary or steno or receptionist girl, talk about jute, tea, steel and iron–coal, curse the seven forefathers of the government who imposes tax after tax after tax and proceed towards the dinner hall. Whenever they get time, one steno asks another, 'What is your salary? How many times have you had abortions? How much did this sari of yours cost?'

Nirmal doesn't have a steno. He knows how to type, and he can type 80 words per minute. His affection for the rhythmic clatter of his typewriter matches the fondness he holds for the nimbleness of his fingers.

The waiter brought a flask of coffee and a tin of cigarettes. Engrossed in his work, Nirmal remained awake throughout the night, alternating between standing by the window and sitting at the table. His focus was unwavering as he meticulously crafted diverse charts on long strips of white and green paper—charts, graphs and diagrams, intertwining lines and numbers with purpose and precision. An unflagging chessboard of straight and zigzagging lines. Paper schemes. Company. Limited company. Public limited company. Capital, shares, interest, board of directors. Partner. Dummy. Blueprint. Tax, fund, income tax, black fund. An unflagging chessboard of straight and zigzagging streaks.

Nirmal Padmavat was engaged in the assessment of others' incomes and social status.

He was supposed to meet Prabhas Babu at 7 a.m. sharp and the outcome of this meeting held the potential to elevate him to the pinnacle of the city's social hierarchy. Prabhaschandra Niyogi was well acquainted with the path leading to this prominent position; he had forged his own route to success.

Nirmal had already decided in New York that he would meet Niyogi first thing on his return to the country. Prabhaschandra Niyogi—as if he had heard this name only in his dreams. Hearing the name woke him up. There was an intense blue light adorning the window frame, and within it, Nirmal perceived the name 'Prabhaschandra Niyogi' written in the Devanagari script. Nirmal had never heard of Niyogi's name before this incident. But this miracle cannot be termed a 'miracle' or a 'vision'. Because miracles are always spiritual in nature, like Savitri reaching the doorway to Heaven by questioning and praying to Yamaraj. The miracle witnessed by Nirmal was just a commercial miracle.

The Hirashah Publishing Company had published an illustrated book on thick art paper in English, titled *Who Is Who in Calcutta Business Industry*; and for the first time in this book, Nirmal had read about the life and business activities of Prabhaschandra Niyogi. In his early life, Nirmal was a draftsman at a famous firm that built houses, bridges, factories and offices. But he used to go to the India Centre every day. He would visit the hotels where the rich and the noble of India used to stay in New York. He would go to the library and read his country's newspapers. In the snippets he perused, Nirmal learned of Harlalka Company's inauguration of three factories in South India, the Income Tax Department's heightened scrutiny on the Dalmia Group and the owners of Vishveshwari Cotton Mills ending the three-month-long strike of their workers.

Nirmal used to collect all sorts of news, trivial as well as big, about every Indian industrialist–capitalist who came to America. Native capitalists had not yet started joint capital business on a large scale by forging alliances with foreign capitalists. However, the advent of foreign capital in the country resulted in American industrialists, who wanted to augment their capital in the countries of East Asia, looking at India with greedy eyes. On a government level, American machines and American engineers for maintaining and upkeep of the machines started pouring into India. Machines and their spare parts came from all over the world, including the USA, Russia, the UK, and West and East Germany. Prabhaschandra Niyogi had never been to America. In a special congregation at Calcutta's Chamber of Commerce, Niyogi had said, 'Earlier we were only slaves to the Queen of Britain, but now, by establishing the capital of different countries in our country, we will become slaves of all those countries by giving them machines, technical education, war weapons, ships, tractors, motor vehicles and medicines, and by timely supplying wheat, dry milk and books; and in return, they would buy our economy and business system. All the capital and engineering engaged in our country's industry, business and factories should be from our country.'

Industrialist Prabhas Babu, the visionary who foresaw these developments, had refrained from forming alliances with any foreign power or capital. Like the old feudal lords, he had a monopoly in his business. By virtue of news and reporters, Nirmal knew about Prabhas Babu as much as the other industrialists of Clive Street, Calcutta. Nirmal knew only one thing more than others that Prabhaschandra Niyogi had taken responsibility for his widowed mother and siblings from the age of eleven or twelve, by working in ordinary hotels, humble shops and small offices.

Nirmal had another valuable source in Kalyani who intently knew every person in India with an annual income above ₹15 lakh. Nirmal knew several languages of his country; he would converse in Gujarati with Daya Mehta and in Assamese with Prashant Barua even in the city of

New York. His ingenuous smile had created a place for him in every house.

The only challenge for him in New York was that, because of his extremely dark complexion, he was often mistaken for a Black American. He had to face the wrath of the White public in White hotels and White bar houses. It was only when the public ensured that this man was from India, was an Indian and not a Black American, that they would feel embarrassed, and ask for an apology. These circumstances had made him tolerant and restrained. As such, he was very fierce; he could not tolerate dishonesty and false pride. Once in defence of a Black woman, he had physically confronted two White Americans. When summoned to court, he had said, 'Even if any Black woman is insulted in front of me today, just because of the colour of her skin, I will break the head of the perpetrator. I am a black man myself. I am black! And I don't consider blackness to be ugly or criminal.'

Niyogi is a short, extremely obese, bald man. His face flushes easily, attesting to an abundance of blood circulation. A noticeable feature is his slightly crooked nose, appearing as if it has been broken in the middle, a characteristic that he doesn't attempt to conceal with the frame of his eyeglasses. Despite this apparent ruggedness, his demeanour is surprisingly soft and sentimental. His eyes, cold and languid, seem to extend from beneath a snowy expanse. Also, despite the age of sixty-five, Niyogi is agile and smart. He never falls sick.

Niyogi had set foot in the share market at the age of eighteen. He comes from a family of limited means. Niyogi's father had to go to jail for misappropriation of funds and died there, never to return. How would he have faced his wife was his father's predicament. Niyogi's mother, residing in a realm of prayers and devotion to saints, coped with the hardships through spiritualism. Niyogi had a younger sister as well, Sarla. Despite wearing a frock, Sarla appeared older and more mature, spending her days visiting neighbours' houses. Sometimes she would demand money, whether eight anna or even four anna. Despite her mind being all over the place, Sarla was popular among the older residents of the locality. Apparently, she had never committed any sins; in fact, the concept of sin never seemed to have crossed her mind. She would sit beside the elders to keep them company and occasionally relieve them of physical discomfort by massaging their fingers and backs.

Despite that, Prabhaschandra Niyogi showered his maximum affection on this half-mad sister of his, who never could straighten her ways. She kept getting pregnant each year and in the process became insane. After losing her mind, she returned to her brother's place. Became a widow. She had five kids, all of whom died within a span of six years.

She now lives in Kashi and takes holy dips in the Ganga and offers prayers at Shiva temples. Niyogi says, 'In the twentieth century, a woman more unfortunate than Sarla has not been born.' By virtue of this acknowledgement, he consistently sends her a monthly cheque of ₹800. However, this strength to issue a cheque has come to him after a long struggle of twenty-six years.

When the Second World War commenced, Niyogi left the stock market. He started a military contracting business. Sending food grains, clothes, uniforms, tents, entertainment items and girls to the military cantonments spread across the borders of Burma, Nepal, Sikkim and Nagaland was his responsibility. During this period, whenever Prabhaschandra would become displeased with any woman, he would find a pretext to send her to the battlefront.

In times of war, the greatest hardships befall the farmers

and urban women. As farmers take up arms and join the conflict, the fields lie fallow, village gossip fails to enliven the hearths, and even on days of rituals and festivals, drums and cymbals remain silent. The women, devoid of tears and sobs, instead, smear ink on their faces and move to the city, where they roam naked in the markets.

This is what happened in the last World War. Niyogi regularly dispatched thirty thousand chickens and chicks, fifteen thousand bottles of rum and twenty-five nurses every week to the brave soldiers at the Burma Front. Akbar Allahabadi wrote about these nurses, 'The nurses know everything, the doctors are confused... For the sake of one affair, the whole world is confused...

On the day of Japan's downfall, when the news of the American atomic bomb being dropped on Hiroshima was broadcast, Prabhaschandra Niyogi's Munshiji tallied the calculations and confidently proclaimed that no moneylender would hesitate to acknowledge him as a millionaire. In response to this, Niyogi had replied, 'Munshiji, summon the dancer, Kamala Devi. She will grace us with her presence tonight.'

Kamala used to be the most celebrated dancer and singer in Calcutta in those days. Niyogi had once seen her on the stage of Moti Mahal theatre many years ago, and he had decided to invite her when he became a millionaire.

After joining the small queue of millionaires, Prabhaschandra Niyogi for the first time in his life got a taste of the 'other woman'. Prior to this, Niyogi had never allowed himself the luxury of rest and sleep. Even when the sensation surfaced, he possessed an immense strength to suppress it beneath the weight of his responsibilities. Consequently, Niyogi found solace in the pursuit of silver and gold, prioritizing wealth over repose. The silver and gold bullion markets emerged as the epicentre of Indian life in the twentieth century, the very heart and soul of existence, where the infusion of vitality into life's essence commenced. Niyogi, having understood these dynamics since childhood, applied his intelligence with adept skill.

Four

Nirmal Padmavat resembled one of those black idols of Greek warriors, while Prabhaschandra Niyogi emanated the essence of the white idols of Greek philosophers. Neither of them was modern, nor did they keep themselves up-to-date.

Nirmal was sitting in the drawing room when Niyogi, dressed in a white pajama and white silk kurta, white attire and a whiteness draped around his face, arrived. Nirmal stood up and smiled. His bright white teeth were shining. Niyogi, eschewing formalities, cut straight to the point, posing a direct question, 'I received your cable from New York. You were there on the fourth day!'

'I only came yesterday. I will stay here from now. I had written to you...' Nirmal replied. Niyogi gazed at him sharply. He wanted to scrutinize Nirmal to ensure that the latter wasn't pretending. There was a firmness in his voice and honesty in his eyes. He wasn't sceptical; in fact, he believed and had faith in his own strength. 'I haven't read your letter... Tell me, what's the matter?' he asked sweetly.

'You must not have found the time.'

'I don't have time... Look, I have a 9 p.m. flight to Bombay. Whatever you want to say... What's the matter?'

'I know you are going to Bombay and that you will be back on Saturday.'

'What is the matter?'

Despite Niyogi's clear indifference, Nirmal refused to be belittled. He stood his ground, not accepting Niyogi's tone as an insult. He said, 'I'll tell you. I will take 10–15 minutes of your time, not much. You please listen to me...'

Nirmal was born in a small village in North Bihar. After his father's demise, his mother sold the ancestral house and eloped with a lorry driver. He was a boy of only ten at that time. Surprisingly, Nirmal didn't feel sorrow for his mother's departure; instead, the pain stemmed from the sale of the family home. He rationalized her leaving as her needing a man, that it was fair for her to go, but the perplexing question remained—why did she take the house with her?

After running away from the village, Nirmal went straight to Karachi. From Karachi to Lahore. He earned his livelihood by washing dishes in a Muslim hotel in Sialkot. Then he became a waiter in the same hotel. He would get the evening shift from four till midnight, waiting tables. 'Bring the *kaleji*, bring the *tandoori*.' 'O black boy, what are you doing, bring a packet of Kainchi cigarettes.' He had befriended a maulana who sold perfume and was very fond of the latter's green beard.

However, one day, Maulana Israrul Haq invited him to his room, and once there, Nirmal brandished a knife—a vegetable cutter. Following this unsettling incident, no man dared to take him to their room. Maulana said to Fateh Singh, the owner of the hotel, in front of all the customers, 'I swear, this boy of yours is the son of a bastard, Badshah. I treated him like a son, my friends, and he threatened me with a knife...' People sitting at the tables of the hotel reiterated, 'Today's children are like this, Maulana! They don't even value their father's love!'

Nirmal would juggle his job at the hotel in the evenings

with selling newspapers in the morning and afternoon. He would ingeniously craft paper bags, toys and flowers from old newspapers. After a few days, he started a newspaper stall on Azad Road. In those days Azad Road was named Isabella Road. Isabella was the wife of an English commissioner. Notably, Isabella was apprehended by Bhagat Singh's associates on this very road, and that self-respecting English girl chose not to return to her husband. Rumour has it that she joined forces with the same revolutionaries who had detained her.

'I have never been to Sialkot,' Prabhaschandra Niyogi said. 'But it is pure coincidence that I met Isabella Rutherford, right here in Calcutta. In those days I used to work with Seth Jamnadas Harnamdas. Isabella had come to collect donations for her Shakti Ashram. Do you know, Nirmal? After deserting the revolutionaries, that English girl fell prey to witchcraft.'

Nirmal started smiling. 'I know. I know everything about Isabella,' he said, as if reminiscing about a past romance.

Along with a small stall of newspapers and magazines, he also opened a tea stall. He himself started studying Urdu and Hindi with the help of a Maulvi. At his shop, Congressmen, revolutionaries, Muslim League leaders, Arya Samajis, all would sit side by side drinking tea and discussing politics. However, one day, the police arrived, claiming that Nirmal's shop served as a base for revolutionary activities. Materials used for crafting crude bombs were reportedly seized from Nirmal, resulting in a four-year sentence for him.

In jail, Nirmal found himself in the company of thieves, dacoits and public leaders. It was here that he grasped the importance of acquiring knowledge and experience. Prompted by the question of what he truly wanted, Nirmal embarked on a journey of studying economics and history under the guidance of Congress leaders. He realized that the common goal of law, religion, science and politics was to bring happiness and prosperity to humanity. Any system or regime that impoverished and crippled people needed to be dismantled. To Nirmal, Aristotle and Karl Marx stood as examples of perfect individuals, embodying ideals that inspired him during his time in jail.

After his release, Nirmal went to Bombay. He travelled the whole world as a waiter in the canteen of a cargo ship. Tokyo, Hong Kong, Peking, Moscow, Warsaw, Budapest, Berlin, Vienna, Paris. During his voyages, he witnessed the ravages of the World War, observing Europe being torn apart in both the Great War and the Second World War. He also encountered the aftermath of the rogue Nazi regime in Germany, with the infamous Berlin Wall serving as a poignant symbol of human folly. Soldiers from Britain, France and Germany found it challenging to reintegrate into civilian life. The whole of Europe seemed to be walking on broken glass, on pavements crammed with corpses.

In Paris, older prostitutes and affluent widows immersed themselves in the melancholy tales of Kafka and the old poems of Paul Valéry, shedding tears for a bygone era that once boasted of Napoleon and a mighty queen. Meanwhile, intellectuals in Oxford and London, seeking solace from the tumultuous world, recited verses from the Bible beneath the shadow of beer bottles. Nirmal, having spent considerable time in America, decided to pause his travels. It was now time to sit somewhere for a while and think about building a house—a place adorned with pots of seasonal flowers on the balcony.

The goddess of liberty was standing on the beach of New York with a flaming torch in her hands, the crown on her head adorned with spikes representing rays of the sun.

Nirmal was mesmerized. When he met Isabella on the porch of the Ridge Hotel for the first time in his life, he considered his dark complexion his strength and that it served his self-interest. While talking to Kalyani, he realized that Bernard Shaw was not wrong and had written the true story of the daunted fourteen-fifteen-year-old girl, Cleopatra, and fifty-five-year-old warlord, Julius Caesar, hiding under the shield of the Sphinx... Nirmal was enchanted and intoxicated.

Nirmal studied America's economy in this state of intoxication. He tried to study and comprehend things pertaining to labour, production, capital, distribution, dividends, free trade and calculation of government taxes. As he surveyed the high offices, he couldn't help but notice the seemingly insignificant individuals who lacked a clear understanding of their existence. These men were oblivious to the reasons behind their life and death, as well as the nature of their sins.

'I want to do business with you, even though I do not have the capital. You don't have to help me; just negotiate a business deal with me,' Nirmal Padmavat said in clear words.

On hearing this, lines of anger or ennui that Nirmal could not comprehend started floating in Niyogi's stone-like lifeless eyes. However, Niyogi did not say anything, just kept gazing into his eyes. Nirmal sat up straight and said, 'I need a loan of thirty thousand rupees from your bank. I will return all the money with interest within two months. I need this money within a week.'

After a long pause, Prabhaschandra Niyogi finally smiled, lovingly, for the first time. His smile grew wider and broadened. Nirmal felt as if Niyogi's smile had filled the whole room simultaneously with light and smoke—and this smoke was emanating from incense sticks rather than the coal furnace. Isabella once said to Nirmal, 'Nobody is a stranger to us, Nirmal. If not in this birth, then in a previous birth, or even in a birth before that, in one way or the other, we are all familiar with each other. Without a cosmic connection, no encounter is possible.'

Nirmal recognized this typical smile. Isabella used to smile like this, and her face used to blossom like morning flowers. But after a moment, the morning flowers withered. Niyogi posed a question as straight and strong as a rod of steel, 'Can someone provide surety on your behalf? Any security?'

'Except for my brain, I have no capital, no surety,' Nirmal did not boast. He humbly hung his head, sitting with his left foot perched on his right. His face turned stubborn; his eyes sparkled. He became alert and Niyogi felt intimidated by his facial expression. 'Why do you need such a large amount? What will you do?' Niyogi questioned carefully. Nirmal wanted to hear this question exactly, instead of the question about the surety.

However, he did not reveal that due to the impulsiveness of the owners, dishonesty of the employees, and workers' strike, the National Jute Mill had been closed for the past two years. Many machines have been sold off. That there was a loan on the company. Nirmal Padmavat would buy this jute mill on lease by paying fifteen thousand rupees in advance. He has checked the accounts and prepared the middlemen. Nirmal replied, 'I will engage in business; I cannot say more at the moment!'

A hush fell over the drawing room, and amid the silence, Nirmal, armed with calculations, maintained his composure. Meanwhile, Niyogi engaged in his own calculations, assessing the man before him—his mind, his value. Niyogi began to pace around the room, contemplating why this man had singled him out. The carpet is patterned with beautiful flowers and leaves, and a picture of Lord Jagannath adorns the wall. The film actresses in the calendars look ugly with their smiles for soap, oil and toothpaste advertisements. An old servant entered, bearing two glasses of sherbet. Nirmal lit a cigarette, and Niyogi kept smiling while navigating the flood of thoughts going through his mind. After a brief pause, Niyogi finally uttered, 'Do you even know how much trouble I am in? Do you?'

Nirmal was well-acquainted with the challenges Prabhaschandra Niyogi was facing. The industry minister was at odds with Niyogi, and income tax officials were relentlessly pursuing him. A strike was causing disruptions at the Prabhaschandra Cotton Mill, and the government had appointed a 'receiver' for the Durgavati Trust. However, these issues, though significant, paled in comparison to the deeper, more personal crisis. Nirmal was privy to a more profound concern. Prabhaschandra Niyogi's youngest daughter, a mere six-year-old, was motherless. Ms Sapna Sarkar, the nurse hired to care for her, levelled grave accusations against Niyogi, including defamation, forgery, impropriety and rape. These serious charges led to three simultaneous cases filed against Niyogi in the Bankshall Court. As a result, the reputation of both Prabhaschandra Niyogi and Niyogi's West Bengal Bank suffered in the market. The share prices of West Bengal Bank plummeted from ₹85 per share to ₹30. Fearing a potential collapse, businessmen were settling their accounts in West Bengal Bank, worsening the situation. Nirmal was keenly aware of the gravity of this fundamental problem.

'Marry Sapna Sarkar. She is a widow, she will agree. She'll withdraw the cases if you do so. Consequently, you'll earn a good name in the society. Marrying a widow will position you as a social reformer. You'll regain your credibility. You'll lose nothing by making her your wife. The singular good that you are doing is, you are buying the shares of your own bank under false names at a low cost. Continue doing this. The rate of shares will shoot up to ₹100 in a few days. Something worth ₹30 will be sold for ₹100. You understand this, don't you?' Each word from Nirmal Padmavat was carefully strung on the bow of his lips and shot towards Niyogi like a verbal arrow. Following this volley of words, Nirmal fell silent, focusing on stubbing the cigarette in the ashtray. This world operates in a certain way. Wherever you lead, it follows with its head bowed, much like a herd of goats. The key is strength, and even more crucial is channelling that strength in the right direction.

Prabhaschandra Niyogi sat on one edge of the sofa and cast his eyes downward. He was not thinking of Nirmal but about Sapna Sarkar. Niyogi exhibited a vulnerability, someplace, somewhere, that Sapna had keenly perceived, and now Nirmal himself began to comprehend it as well.

A woman's body is not a justification for dismantling the walls of solitude. Niyogi hadn't fallen in love with the smart and well-dressed nurse caring for his little girl. He was alone, leading a lonely life. When Sapna Sarkar brought him a cup of hot coffee, or sometimes sleeping pills, it felt good. All of this felt good to him.

When a person, beyond the role of a mere servant or cook, starts serving as a true family member, their departure can evoke overwhelming emotions. Before retiring for the night, Sapna would come into the bedroom, cover him with a duvet, administer medicines, turn off the lights and bid him an affectionate goodnight. All these gestures brought a sense of comfort. It was the accumulation of such small pleasures that gradually eased Prabhaschandra's mind and body to her presence.

And then one day Sapna told him that she didn't want to remain a nurse. She wanted to pursue a career in the film industry. Niyogi had harboured a lot of hatred for film stars and films over the years. He never went to the cinema. He decided not to help Sapna Sarkar in this endeavour. He had decided that if she uttered the name of films again, or the names of film companies, Niyogi would find a new nurse for his daughter. 'If you can't make me a film star, then marry me,' Sapna declared one fine day, catching him off guard. He was totally startled.

However, when Nirmal Padmavat expressed the same sentiment, he felt neither amazed nor infuriated. Instead, he decided to help Nirmal settle down in Calcutta.

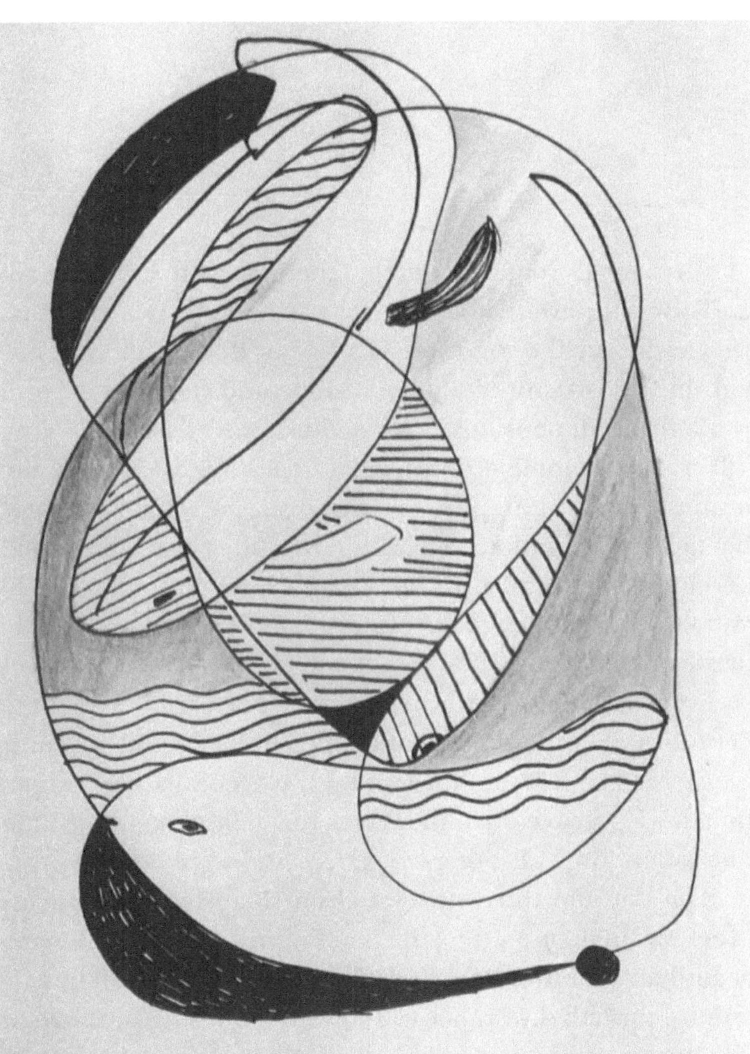

Five

$\mathcal{E}$very small road eventually merges with a big road. Following every small intersection, there is a big one. After every small floor, there is a bigger floor. Buildings rise high in this structured pattern. Scope and function expand in all three dimensions. The acquisition of National Jute Mill is now complete. Nirmal Padmavat, proficient in the businesses of cotton, jute, tea and iron, personally oversees the factory operations of Miller & Miller Co. Renowned merchants of Burrabazar and Cotton Street affirm, 'Nirmal Padmavat possesses a profound understanding of the market.'

From one profit another capital is accrued. From the second capital, the third profit is generated. If the accounts are correct, if the rules for writing the accounts are correct, then it is possible to build even the tallest building: one that towers over all others.

The day the thirty-storey Kalyani Mansion on Princess Street was inaugurated by the chief minister of West Bengal, Dr Bidhan Chandra Roy, he said while cutting the ribbon, 'I am sure this tall skyscraper will solve the housing problem of our huge metropolis. On behalf of the people of Calcutta, I extend my gratitude to the famous industrialist, Shri Nirmal Babu for constructing Kalyani Mansion for this specific purpose, which is a noble cause, to say the least.' Nirmal's dream, perhaps his first and final, finally materialized.

This dream was sowed on the same day his mother had sold their house and eloped with a lorry driver and the new owner of the house had shoved Nirmal and his little dog out of the house. Nirmal had experienced eviction not only from his own home but others' as well, numerous times, throughout his life. However, these adversities did not break his spirit. He endured humiliation with maturity and tolerance, all with the hope that someday he would stand at the threshold of his 'Kalyani Mansion'.

Once, Kalyani had taken him to her room in Shangri-La Hotel in New York. Inserting the key into the keyhole, she had said, 'Now you go, Nirmal Babu! Now you go! You must go!' Nirmal had quietly turned back and returned to the lift. But he had returned, just to come back once again!

Kalyani had come to America to study medicine; although, she couldn't continue her studies. Money ceased to come from home. The issue of 'foreign exchange' arose. Her mother wrote letters, sent telegrams and tried to allure her in various ways—'Kalyani, my daughter, you have to come back.' Despite the persistent calls to come back, Kalyani continued to wander freely, like an untethered kite, across New York, California and Los Angeles. Unyielding, she refused to be restrained, as her soul was captivated by the uncharted and independent skies of this new-found free world.

This world is a realm of both wilderness and newspapers, where individuals navigate through the narratives and stories that surround their own lives. People strip off wherever they want to, where nudity is not blasphemy. It is also not sacrilegious to jump off the Brooklyn Bridge to die. It's dark in the settlements of Manhattan. One sees people sitting on tabourets in small bars that are dimly lit and filled with cigarette smoke. They are talking about Indian hermits and Chinese hotels. A woman bangs her glass on the table and, lifting the hem of her skirt and stooping, climbs atop the table and starts dancing to the wild tunes of drums and accordion, like Silvana Mangano and Sophia Loren. Mambo! Black music…the music of the Spanish Gypsies! Ra-ra-rum, ra-ra-rum-rum-ra-rum, ra-ra-rum, rum-rum! Sherry…sherry bacoo rum, high elm! High elm! Sherry bacoo rum!—oh my love, you have not tasted the sherry cask finished rum, then how would you love?—Ra-ra-rum, ra-ra-rum!

This gypsy music drove Kalyani crazy. She would wander around after drinking the aged sherry rum. Though lacking in funds, she possessed a golden diary adorned with a plethora of phone numbers and addresses—both old and new. She worked as a model in fashion shows. Many painters and professional photographers celebrated the contours and movements of her body. Kalyani was the only woman from India in New York who did not cease to be visible. Standing in the queue of American models, she looked radiant with her million-dollar smile.

Kalyani had to sit next to Nirmal Padmavat at the dinner table at a function organized by the Indian Embassy. There was no exchange of words or formal introductions between them. Amidst the crowd of strangers, these two individuals remained strangers. However, once Nirmal Padmavat had set his eyes on Kalyani, he could not get his eyes off her. He tried to find Kalyani's name and address in the telephone directory but to no avail.

Suddenly, one fine evening, their paths crossed in a theatre on Broadway. Kalyani was standing in the lounge, engaged in conversation with a Sikh man. Nirmal was alone, gazing at the pictures on a board on the walls. The moment Kalyani spotted Nirmal, she swiftly approached him with a genuine smile of affection and friendship. Almost hugging him, she said, 'I was waiting for you, darling—dear! I was waiting! I was…!'

A question arose in Nirmal's mind, *Has this woman lost her mind?* But he just started smiling. The Sikh man, wearing an expensive suit from 'Sears' and with a well-groomed beard, joined Nirmal and said, 'I have come from Amritsar. I run the roadways bus service there. Nice to meet our people here. It is very good to meet people from our country. I met Deviji at Kristen Hotel only two days ago.'

'Rescue me! This man will devour me!' she whispered in Nirmal's ears in Bengali. Nirmal understood as he knew the language. With swift readiness, he prepared himself, as he was not one to dither. Smilingly, but in a very stern tone, he told the Sardar, 'I don't want to get into introductions, I am sorry… Let's go, Kalyani. We should go in! We have to go in!'

Holding Kalyani's hand, Nirmal Padmavat headed towards the theatre house's balcony. While climbing the stairs he asked Kalyani, 'How many dollars have you charged this Sethji from Amritsar? Hundred dollars? Two hundred?' Kalyani freed her arm and laughed sarcastically. She climbed the stairs hurriedly while laughing all the way. When Nirmal came close to her, she said, 'Why do you care; do you need your commission?'

Nirmal Padmavat harboured no interest in a commission; he simply wished to familiarize himself with Kalyani and comprehend her carnal aspirations. As they paused near the ticket room, Kalyani paid for both their tickets. Nirmal asserted, 'I don't want a commission.'

The people around them started staring. Like wheat spikelets, ivory-skinned, full-bodied Kalyani! And Nirmal Padmavat, like a cliff of black stones. Kalyani adorned her bun with flowers like Keralite women and was wearing a bright red silk sari. 'If you don't want a commission, then what do you want?' Kalyani asked coyly.

Within the last two days, Kalyani had taken 250 dollars from Sardar Nihaal Singh. And she had already spent the money in the past two days. She failed to save money for rainy days because every day was a 'rainy day' for her. If she had money, she sat in a nice and lonely pub, drinking port or sherry, and remained immersed in her fantasies. And if she didn't have money, she used to smoke Pall Mall cigarettes, lie in bed and sleep after drinking any cheap alcohol. She knew thousands of people in the city, yet she did not have any friends. Most of the time she stayed alone. But when the hotel's debt increased, and there was no money to bring the washed clothes from the laundry, it was time for her to take out her most expensive sari and blouse.

She would exit her room by putting on light make-up—alone but fully decked up. She meets a Sardar Nihaal Singh somewhere in The Plaza, or on Madison Avenue, or Times Square. As introductions are made, the person who comes in contact with Kalyani is taken aback by her dialogue and mannerisms.

In short, this is her profession. Although she despises it, she is not aware of any other kind of work. She could not become a film star. And even on Broadway, no suitable roles emerged. Briefly, on television, she portrayed roles of an Indian princess, an Indian girl studying in America, an Indian air hostess, an Indian housewife, and after a few days, she became a model. She is still a model and even now, she works in blue films sometimes.

Kalyani has made a detailed note of prominent facets and components of contemporary American culture. Written in beautiful and clear alphabets, she has hung this list on the wall in a corner.

1. Blue films
2. Jazz music and Black girls
3. Dale Carnegie
4. Plays by Tennessee Williams
5. Yellow pages
6. Marilyn Monroe
7. Pubs and shady coffeehouses
8. Fear of communism, and
9. Skyscrapers

'Then what do you want from me?' Kalyani asked again. This time, she was not shy. Rather, she was rejoicing in the dual meaning of her question.

'I don't want anything. I just want to know how many times this Sardarji has—' Nirmal, on the verge of saying something harsh, stopped. He did not complete the sentence.

But Kalyani understood. She felt insulted and bowed her face in a display of self-perceived inadequacy before Nirmal. She wasn't that diminutive; perhaps, it was the towering integrity of Nirmal Padmavat that cast a shadow on her. She found herself unable to meet Nirmal's gaze. A fourteen- or fifteen-year-old boy with an usherette tray displaying cigarettes came and stood in front of them.

Kalyani wanted to buy cigarettes, but she resisted. She feared that smoking in Nirmal's presence might reveal her inner turmoil; her hands would quiver, and the cigarette might slip from her grasp. Nirmal bought a packet of Pall Mall; he knew Kalyani smoked this very brand.

That day at the party in the Indian Embassy, Nirmal had observed Kalyani smoking a cigarette and mingling with everyone while holding a small glass of cocktail. She prowled from table to table, smiling, stroking the backs of her acquaintances. Her eyes sparkled like a goldfish when she laughed.

Nirmal had never gotten the chance to see this glow from up close. He had certainly seen women, but never from close quarters. None had ever approached him so intimately, asking what he desired and how he desired it.

After this meeting at Broadway, he started meeting Kalyani often. She had shared the address of her hotel with him. She would often come to meet him whenever he called. Both would spend time in some cheap pub and discuss the happenings in and around their country and city. Mostly Kalyani would do the talking. Nirmal would remain silent. Once, Kalyani fell ill. She left her hotel and went to stay with a friend. Many months passed and, one fine day, she herself called Nirmal. After finishing his office work, Nirmal went to meet her.

She was waiting for Nirmal in a big restaurant in the Manhattan area. She wasn't alone; Pratap had accompanied her. They were drinking beer sitting at the table near the door in the hall of the Walrus Restaurant. Nirmal went and stood beside them. Kalyani, at that time, was busy laughing at Pratap's remarks. She couldn't contain her amusement, even when she spotted Nirmal. She appeared fuller and more radiant than before, clad in an attire tighter than ever.

Pratap was the new heir to an aristocratic *zamindar* family and had arrived with his uncle to gain insights into the business and establish connections in the international iron and steel market. Despite his talent and regal demeanour, Pratap, a reserved and shy young man, appeared remarkably youthful and fresh in the presence of Kalyani.

After the introductions, Kalyani said, 'I'm going to marry Pratap. The wedding will take place in San Diego. Then we'll both come back to California and...! She extended her right hand towards Nirmal. A precious stone sparkled on her middle finger—a big, uneven piece of topaz.

Nirmal found it hard to believe that Kalyani had invited him to this faraway restaurant merely to share this seemingly trivial information and introduce him to this seemingly insignificant young man. *Surely there is some other matter as well,* he contemplated. He was right indeed! Kalyani wanted Nirmal Padmavat to meet Pratap's uncle the next morning and tell him about the entire situation. Nirmal smirked after hearing this proposal. It looked like Kalyani harboured intentions of blackmail. She was holding Pratap's emotions in her grip and was now seeking financial gain from Pratap's uncle in exchange for this emotional manipulation.

Pratap, at the tender age of twenty or twenty-two, experienced Kalyani as perhaps the first significant woman in his life, within whose embrace he allowed himself to freely unwind. Pratap emptied a tall glass of beer and said, 'Nirmal, Brother, for me, this is a question of life or death. My uncle is the trustee of my land and property. But now I am an adult. If he wants to stop me, then I'll create a ruckus on returning to my country. It won't take me long to elope to America by selling my entire property at throwaway prices—not even a day's delay. But I would still request you to try so that there is no obstacle in our path. If you're able to convince Uncle, then I'll make you the director of my company. I want to open a steel factory.'

Nirmal felt the urge to burst into laughter as he listened to this entire conversation. He wished to sing the popular song of Mexican peasant women, the one that begins with:

A paper moon,
can be affixed to the sky,
yet, it will always be

bereft of light.
A paper moon,
shall never spread moonbeams,
under no circumstances.

After a little while, Kalyani transitioned Pratap from a tall glass of beer to a sizeable bottle of rum. As the intoxication took its toll, Pratap succumbed to sleep, resting one arm beneath his head, slumbering on the table. It was around ten or eleven in the night. The rabble of travellers had increased in the restaurant. After the Mexican song, Nirmal Padmavat was reminded of these famous lines by T.S. Eliot:

> In the room the women come and go
> Talking of Michelangelo.

He reiterated to the woman sitting on the chair in front of him, 'How young, how humble this boy is, how gentle! Why are you spoiling him? Who is responsible for turning you this savage? You've resorted to crime these days.' Imbued in the purity of milk rather than alcohol, Kalyani cheerfully announced, 'I've booked the best room in Shangri-La Hotel this time. It's a three-bedroom suite.'

Kalyani casually tousled her loosely tied hair, clearly inebriated. The restaurant, in her perception, resembled a ship navigating through vibrant, luminous hues. A young woman of African descent, gripping the microphone, rendered a Spanish song, swaying her jet-black physique to the rhythm. A new poet's freshly composed song unfolded:

> *Bajo mi codo, en mi codo*
> *Bajo mi cama, en mi cama*
> *Bajo mi pie, en mi pie*
> *Bajo mis ojos, en mis ojos*
> *Sí, sí; la he encontrado—*

La perdida llave, llave, llave, llave, llave
Qué pájaro canta esa canción
Llave, llave
Bajo mi codo, en mi codo
*Bajo mi codo!**

Kalyani could decipher the lyrics as she had been to Mexico several times and had roamed in many parts of Latin America. She felt a surge of joy realizing that the dark-skinned woman on stage could empathize with her inner turmoil. Kalyani had discovered the elusive key, and it was none other than Pratap.

Nirmal asked in a tranquil and soft tone, 'Don't you ever miss your country, your home? You had come here to study medicine, but ironically, you've fallen sick yourself.'

Kalyani was startled. Suddenly she felt as if she found a carcass walking right under her nose. In fear and trepidation, she asked Nirmal, 'Whose country? Whose home?... And I am not sick. Do I look sick? Don't I look healthier than before?'

There is no home, no country for Kalyani anymore. She doesn't miss anyone. What's the point of remembering anything?

---

*Under my elbows, in my elbows
Under my bed, in my bed
Under my feet, in my feet
Under my eyes, in my eyes
Yes, yes; I've found yet again—
The lost key, key, key, key, key,
Which bird croons this song
Key, key
Under my elbows, in my elbows
Under my elbows!
  —Diane Wakoski

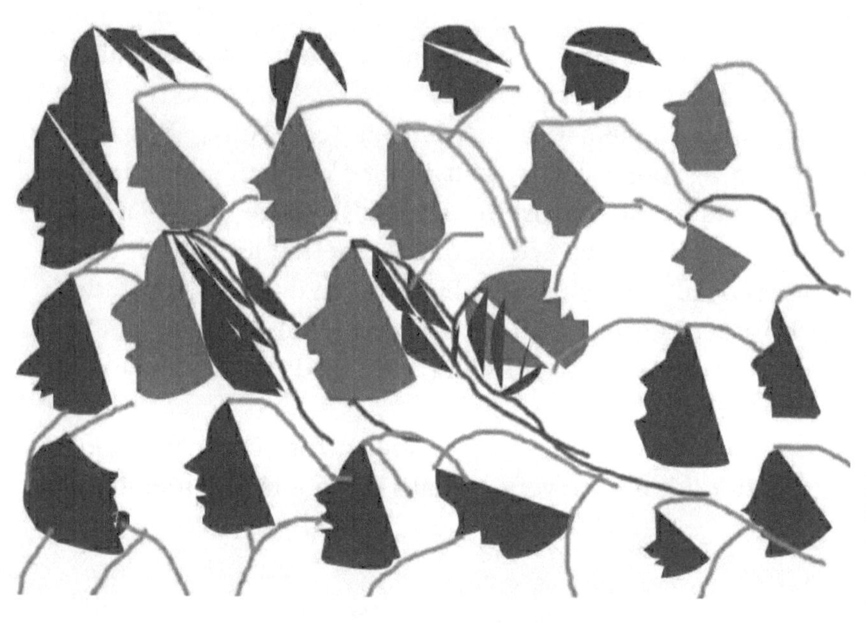

Six

*P*ratap's astute uncle proved to be more adept than Kalyani in the intricate game of manipulation. As Pratap's intoxication subsided, he regained his composure. However, Kalyani, driven by her own financial necessities, gradually adopted a more hostile and self-centred demeanour towards Pratap.

Nirmal Padmavat took a brief leave from his office to visit Kalyani after two to three weeks. Upon arrival, he discovered Kalyani restlessly pacing through her three-bedroom suite. For the first time in life, she yearned to venture out, hire a taxi, but had no money in her purse. She had sold her car just two days ago, yet she was broke. An old acquaintance had come to see Kalyani that morning, but nothing worked out. She was so debilitated and dishevelled that she couldn't even muster the strength to leave her bed for this old acquaintance. The man continued talking for a while, eventually realizing that she was not in good shape.

Kalyani could not stop him. He retreated, promising to visit her again. Kalyani remained in bed until late afternoon. She failed to find the strength to get up and wash her face. She had spent the previous night in a cheap nightclub, chattering with a veteran owner of a shoe company.

She had told Mr Hilton that she was the princess of a large kingdom in Rajasthan. But Mr Hilton could see that Kalyani was not a princess. (After all, he oversaw the production of 35 lakh pairs of shoes annually through his company, displaying intelligence in the business realm. Yet, he frequented inexpensive nightclubs, seeking affordable pleasures, only to return to his wife and business afterwards!) Wealthy women don't make the mistake of stepping into this nightclub. It is a venue frequented by those of lesser means.

Despite Kalyani's modern demeanour, Hilton Sahab treated her with disrespect, regarding her as if she were of low standing. His conversation and actions left Kalyani so uninterested that when he suggested visiting her room after midnight for a cup of coffee, she flatly declined. She asserted bluntly, 'I don't drink coffee. Only whisky; though I prefer rum.'

Kalyani returned to the hotel, eschewing Hilton Sahab, drank the remnants of whisky from the bottle in her almirah and dozed off. Before retiring to bed, she contemplated calling Nirmal Padmavat, planning to invite him to her place. She firmly believed that Nirmal was her ultimate saviour, the only person in the world who could rescue her from this bleak and dismal present.

Nirmal visited her room in the late afternoon. He was unaware of the fact that Pratap had returned to Bombay with his uncle, and Kalyani had sold off her car. He was also unaware that, just like Susan Hayward from the film *I'll Cry Tomorrow*, Kalyani also spent her nights wandering on pavements, bars and clubs, in search of alcohol, sleep and the company of a man.

'How much money do you have in your bank?' Kalyani posed her first question to Nirmal. He wasn't prepared for this question. But he took out his passbook from his portfolio bag and handed it over to Kalyani. She took Nirmal's signature on one of the cheques and sent a trustworthy waiter to the bank to encash it. The entire process unfolded in just three sentences and five minutes. Within half an hour, the hotel's waiter brought the money.

While keeping the amount of $1,250 in her drawer, Kalyani experienced an epiphany. Merely this morning, she lacked the funds even to procure poison. Yet, this man had swiftly altered the course of her life. The lingering question persisted: *What did this man desire? What was his intent?*

Signs of sloth and recklessness began to emanate from Kalyani's eyes. She generously tipped the waiter and said, 'Get lunch for us! And, for drinks…!' When the waiter left, she wrapped her hands around Nirmal in a close embrace and planted a kiss. However, this intimate act did not arouse Nirmal. His lips remained cold and inert.

Releasing her arms from Nirmal's neck, she approached the radiogram and placed an LP record of a famous Mambo tune. She began to dance like a gypsy, snapping her fingers to the beat of the music. However, Nirmal remained absent-minded, lost in the recollections of his village and his troubled past. His thoughts drifted to his mother eloping with a lorry driver, the pet dog he once had and the daily threats from his Chachaji to throw him out of the house. He was immersed in memories of days gone by.

Nirmal had never experienced the love and affection of either a man or a woman in his life. He couldn't evolve into a complete human being; perhaps he remained forever incomplete. His own mother, by eloping and leaving him behind, had contributed to this sense of incompleteness. As she sat in the lorry beside the driver, gazing at the vast world through the front mirror, she bid him adieu forever. Nirmal's understanding of women boiled down to something Emily Dickinson had said, that women did not render support.

But that they did seek a small, strong tree, taking shelter in their arms at all times!

And, what about men? Nirmal didn't know anything about men. Not even about himself. Kalyani had asked him just once; why he handed over his passbook. He didn't have an answer. Perhaps, by entrusting all his savings to Kalyani, he wanted to prove something else. Maybe, in doing so, he sought to demonstrate his love for Kalyani.

In this singular aspect, Nirmal is indecisive, irresolute—uncertain about love. Kalyani was swaying openly to an unscrupulous Mambo number, tapping to the rhythm of applause, and was almost saying 'a small tree should take shelter in my arms, always'. As the record reached its end, Kalyani took a break from the dance. Then she came and sat next to Nirmal Padmavat, squirming and laughing. Perhaps she was happy and content with the thought that there was a man… There is a man who is sitting next to her, who has relinquished all his money, surrendered all his savings to her.

What is the worth of a man? His worth is determined by his purchasing power. His strength is directly proportional to his purchasing power, that is, he is equivalent to his purchasing power, and nothing more! So, Nirmal Padmavat's real worth is $1,250. But now he is just a man—nameless, powerless, not even worth calling a man. Kalyani wondered if she could get this man out of her room; if by raising her brows she commanded in a rigid tone, 'Babu Sahib, you can go now', what would Nirmal do?

Would he commit suicide by jumping from the balcony? Perhaps he wouldn't commit suicide, he might just go insane with anger and hatred, and could kill her… No, Nirmal Padmavat could not commit any of these sins.

For a long time, Kalyani pondered over a multitude of assumptions, contemplating without rhyme or reason. She observed Nirmal minutely, there was no trace of lust, anger, greed, fascination, anything of the like on his face. Like a blank slate, his countenance bore only an ashen colour— no other hues, sentences, words, letters. He was not angry. Perhaps, not even in love.

But...why...then? After a long time today, once again, the same question began to trouble Kalyani. *What does Nirmal want?* His shoulders are tall and broad like a tall statue. Kalyani put her hand on his left shoulder and asked, 'Now?'

'Now, nothing.' Nirmal replied poetically.

'What do we do now?'

'...!'

'Shall we go out somewhere?'

'We can.'

'If you want, we can spend the evening here.'

'...?'

'What does your heart desire? What do you want, tell me? Would you like to go to a pub? Hope you are not regretting it now. I took the money from you because I am in dire need of funds. If I ever get money from somewhere, I will return your $1,250, but only if I get the money.'

'You do not have to return the money.'

'Why not?'

'Neither are you in debt. Nor do I reclaim things once given.'

'But then... then...?'

'Then nothing.'

'...?'

'...'

'What do you want?'

'I don't know.'

Nirmal Padmavat said 'I don't know' with great simplicity, and looked deeper into Kalyani's eyes. She was now solemn and had plunged into deep thoughts. *Nirmal is more cultured and courteous than me, that's why he says, 'I don't know', although he knows.* He knows more than Pratap and Sardar Nihaal Singh. He knows more than anyone in this world as to what exactly he wants, especially, what he seeks from Kalyani.

But this man is merely playing a deceptive role—a melodrama concealing his own deeply buried desires while coaxing others to expose and unveil theirs. Pursing her plump and bright red lips, Kalyani smiled. Her smile was brimming with an uncanny sarcasm.

Nirmal Padmavat could not tolerate this sarcastic gesture. He began to unravel, just like a coiled, wounded snake that unwinds. He blurted out, 'You know it very well, Kalyani, what I want. Then why are you asking me?'

'Just like that.'

'Why?'

'Because I would love to hear it from the horse's mouth. Nirmal, you are from my own country. You will speak in your tongue. Here, I interact not only with Americans but also with Chinese and Africans. Everyone calls me 'white Indian lady', and they want to suck the whiteness out of me. You are from my own country, I know you will not suck it out, rather, you will caress my wounds, and heal my pain...'

Nirmal began to decipher Kalyani's words. He didn't want sarcasm; he sought only love! He loved Kalyani. In his ignorance, he secretly yearned to build a family home around Kalyani that could not be broken by his mother or policemen of Karachi or government jails or gold–silver and paper coins. Nirmal only wanted love. But knowing that Kalyani wanted to give much more than love, Nirmal started falling into the trap of a new desire. Now he was scared and apprehensive. What would happen? How would it be? And for what?

Nirmal Padmavat's mind began to tremble, as if a large rock had been cast into a slumbering river. Ripples of waves emerged from the impact, the circles expanding and distorting, disrupting the surface of the water.

He looked out of the apartment window at the traffic signals and the serpentine queues of cars. He observed people hurrying on the sidewalks. Like every man and woman coming to New York from distant countries to make a mark here, Nirmal too wanted to change the trajectory of his fate. Nirmal too wanted a house, office, cars, bank account, a woman like Kalyani, and the children of this woman that must be his own—Nirmal yearns for that. But Kalyani says, 'Ask for anything you want! I can give you anything.'

'Come on, let's go outside. We'll sit in a restaurant or watch a movie. Today is my day off. Let's go, it's very hot in here.'

'I just crave for warmth. Can't you see the heater is on? Let the evening unfold, and then we can venture out.'

'It doesn't feel comfortable here. Let's go someplace far away. I am feeling claustrophobic here.'

'You are not so wealthy yet, Nirmal, that you feel suffocated in an expensive room like this.' Kalyani laughed out loud, and to excite Nirmal Padmavat, she stretched playfully.

Nirmal stood up. Without asking Kalyani, he closed the door from inside. As soon as the knob was turned, the door was locked. Kalyani kept smiling—what was the need for this? No one here can peek into what happens behind the curtains. Everyone knows. Understands. No one wants to see it. 'Let the door remain open,' she said.

There was a smell of burning flesh in Kalyani's voice. The smell of meat or that of burning rubber. Nirmal felt nauseous. It was extremely hot. The heater was on. The window was open, yet the room was dark. Yellow layers of dim light enveloped everything, as if Nirmal had consumed opium. It seemed as though Kalyani's neck bore not a necklace of fake diamonds, but a real snake with a blue hood.

As if suddenly remembering something important, Nirmal said, 'I am not feeling well, Kalyani! My head is throbbing.' Before entering Kalyani's room, his head had been throbbing with pain. However, he forgot about the headache after entering the room. He forgot everything after seeing Kalyani's voluptuous body, and the pulsating thirst that seemed to emanate from every part of her form.

'Why, what happened? Hope you do not have a fever?' Kalyani thought it essential to show some sympathy. Nirmal is an emotional man (of course, he is!). Without a few words of love, he might retreat. Therefore she said, 'Lay down on the bed, I will apply medicine to your head and neck. You will soon feel better.'

'No, this is not something new. I haven't been keeping well for a very long time now. There is no fever or headache, yet I feel sick. I can't sleep at night, and I keep reading books while lounging. I called you at 2 a.m. last night. The phone rang for a long time, but you did not answer. Perhaps you were somewhere outside. If you were here, I would have come to you...'

'I was right here. I do not answer any calls at night. I feel scared. Some people are after me. I owe money to a few people, and few others want to harass me just like that...' Kalyani said in a sombre tone. She removed her sweater and kept it in her wardrobe. She keeps all her belongings in this wardrobe. She doesn't have many belongings. Few clothes, few books on medical science. A small transistor set. There's also an expensive camera. And her make-up kit. Normally, she doesn't wear make-up. She looks like the goddess of beauty and serenity amidst the American women who wear heavy make-up. Being natural is her magic. She knows the worth of her magic. Kalyani also knows the reason behind Nirmal's severe headache.

'Come to bed. There's nothing to be embarrassed about it. I'll massage your head.' Kalyani held his hand and pulled him towards the bed. She then left to use the washroom. Nirmal sat on the corner of the bed, crouched, head bowed down.

He was intoxicated. His eyes were burning. He felt as if all his veins would burst at once, and his body would be smeared with drops of blood. His legs felt like lead, arms frozen. It was as if he had been placed in a furnace. He wanted to stand on his feet but it was futile. His legs were frozen, as were his arms. His body had turned into an icy block of stone that was beginning to melt slowly.

Kalyani emerged from the bathroom. Nirmal Padmavat saw a pair of bare feet, white as snow. Shapely muscles. Full ankles. Round knees. A yellow glow emanated from the thighs, along with greenish-blue veins. He could not muster the courage to look up.

Advancing towards him, Kalyani said, 'Hang your clothes in the hanger lest they become crumpled. And you must get up from the bed for a moment, let me spread another bedsheet.'

Nirmal got up silently and stood near the almirah. Kalyani took out a red bedsheet and began to spread it on the bed. Nirmal's eyes fell on the reflection of her curved silhouette in the mirror. *Kalyani has a broad back. She has a broad posterior. She is bent over the bed.* Turning her head, she said, 'Why are you staring at me? Come over.'

Nirmal first took off his bush shirt and began searching for an empty hanger. Kalyani's clothes were draped on the hangers, folded saris, blouses and cholis, colourful skirts and scarves, clothes suitable for wearing to dances—frocks, petticoats, lingerie, brassiere. None of the hangers were empty.

Meanwhile, Kalyani had changed the bedsheet and was waiting for Nirmal on the bed. 'If you can't find an empty hanger, hang your clothes on the door, I'll iron them later.'

Then… Nirmal Padmavat discovered a skeleton hanging behind the rows of saris, petticoats and skirts, attached to the cupboard wall. The head was missing, only a mesh of hands, legs and ribcage. No head, nor skin. There was no flesh, only bones. A frame of a man's body, but it was not a man.

Nirmal did not yell, but he shuddered. Then he recalled that Kalyani was a student of medicine. But his fear did not subside. *Kalyani is not a woman, but a demon. She keeps a skeleton behind her clothes and lives in the same room.* Yet, he started taking off his clothes. Such is the intrinsic character of Nirmal. First, he gets scared, and then tries to forget it. He then gets angry with himself and wants to take revenge on others. Revenge for his resentment and fear.

'What have you got hanging in your cupboard?'

'My clothes!'

'Not only clothes, but there's also a skeleton. Where did you get it? You aren't studying medicine anymore. What's the point of keeping it?'

'Oh, why not? Even though in the form of a skeleton, at least I have the companionship of a man.' Kalyani said breezily while pulling Nirmal Padmavat towards the bed. Kalyani's lips were parched. Sweat beads were trickling down her neck. Sweat and sloth. Indolence, intoxication and stifling heat flowed through her veins.

Nirmal was also disconcerted due to the heat. The robust

grip of Kalyani's hands transformed him into a burning mass of fire. He paused but stood there. The skeleton is peeping from behind the row of clothes. It has no head, nor flesh, just bones. On the contrary, Kalyani is lying naked on the bed, replete with flesh. Perhaps she doesn't have a single bone!

Men are intrinsically drawn towards the flesh. The warmth of flesh pulls like a magnet. Blood attracts. Men are savage. They want to scratch and scuff up flesh and muscle.

Nirmal Padmavat dove onto the bed like a starving wolf's cub. He jumped into the burning furnace. Kalyani was grinning from ear to ear, while resisting him, trying to insulate herself from him. She was pandiculating, tossing and turning on the bed. Nirmal realized that Kalyani was much stronger than him. She was lying prostrate on the bed, holding both sides of the bed's frames with her hands and cackling with laughter. Nirmal was unable to drag her towards him. He was tired of trying. Leaning on Kalyani's back, Nirmal was overtired. Kalyani said, chuckling, 'Just with this much strength, you had set out to conquer the world?'

After a while, Kalyani released her hands from the frames of the bed. Suddenly, her eyes caught sight of Nirmal rising on his knees. Nirmal had become as cold as a piece of ice. He was lifeless, the embers in his eyes had extinguished.

'This is the kind of man you are.' Kalyani lost her temper, she started yelling. 'You look like a towering black mountain, but this is what your manhood is all about? That's it? You had come to me just for this much?' she rebuked him. 'Why didn't you tell me before?' Lying on the bed she started beating her hands and feet.

Nirmal got out of the bed and began to put on his clothes, his head bowed down in humiliation. Kalyani continued fuming, 'Never ever show your face to me, Nirmal!

You are not a man, but an insect from hell! Never come to me!'

'I am leaving.' Nirmal Padmavat could speak just one sentence. But he didn't move from his place. He had put on his trousers and shirt.

Kalyani sat up, her legs hanging from the bed. She unclasped the imitation diamond necklace from her neck and threw it near Nirmal's feet. The necklace did not break but scattered on the floor. She said, 'Take this necklace of yours with you. If ever you marry, make your wife wear it.' It had been quite some time since Nirmal had bought this necklace for Kalyani for $25. She was delighted to wear it back then.

Putting the necklace in his pocket, Nirmal came downstairs. However, Kalyani's bellow of rage followed him. The necklace, in his trouser pocket, kept digging into his thigh.

After that day, Nirmal never visited that suite at the Shangri-La Hotel. He never met Kalyani again. Kalyani married Dr Raghuvansh…Kalyani returned to the country… Kalyani passed away.

Such an intersection does not exist where these two fictitious and peculiar people could come together after walking on two different paths.

Seven

*P*riya emerged with the coffee tray in her hand. Doctor uttered in an ecstatic tone, 'You are a lucky man, Nirmal. Priya herself has prepared coffee for you. She doesn't bother to go out of her way and do all these things for anyone, not even for me. Her mother passed away when she was very young.'

Priya had draped herself in a dark yellow Bengal handloom sari, with blue sapphire studs in her ears. A few fringes of her hair cascaded in a deliberately carefree manner, framing her face with a touch of playful elegance. Her countenance exuded a serene innocence.

Her eyes had a glimmer akin to a wild deer brought from the forest and left at the peripheries of the city. But Priya was not a deer of the forest but of the city.

She said, 'Nirmal Sahib, while I've observed Kalyani Mansion from afar, I never got to venture inside the expansive structure. Coincidentally, my mother's name was also Kalyani, and much like your towering building, she too possessed a lofty stature.'

Nirmal felt miserable, as numerous memories of Kalyani chased him. Kalyani…Kalyani Mansion…the past… memories…present…Priya…Priya…Priya. He felt as if all the happiness had been sucked out of his life. The past remains unalterable, impervious to transformation into the present, and vice versa; Nirmal found deep sorrow in this realization, yet he concealed his sadness behind a metaphorical mask. His sadness or his happiness never reflects on his face. The mask took the form of an appearance marked by nonchalance and a serene simplicity.

Embracing desolation as a constant companion, he draped himself in solitude and silence, embodying a steadfast sense of neutrality.

Departing from his small village nestled on the banks of the river Padmavati, Nirmal ventured into the unfamiliar and often perplexing external realm, where ennui soon became a recurring theme. Despair and hard work clung to him like an inescapable embrace, one he couldn't easily extricate himself from. Performing laborious tasks with a mechanical precision reminiscent of a 24/7 automatic machine, he navigated through the challenges of his new reality. People would say that Nirmal was obsessed with money, and they would consider him a patient of neurosis. Nirmal Padmavat, however, never bothered about his madness, his disease or people's perception of him. He continued doing what he had already decided. He continued trying to decipher and decrypt the world around him. He transformed his mind into a bare, sharp sword, poised to cut through the layers of darkness, scattering shards of light at his feet.

Diligence and brilliance by themselves make a man very lonely. He doesn't feel the need to mingle with others. He doesn't have the leisure to even be a part of others' indolence, comfort, hobbies and sensitivities. Hard work doesn't allow him to be a part of the crowd, and talent doesn't let him get lost in the crowd.

Nirmal had made solitude his companion. He was not keen on friendship, rest or even leisure. He didn't have anything except the tall skyscraper at Princess Street. Life follows a unique trajectory, exhibiting reciprocity and embarking on a dynamic journey guided by a predetermined plan. The only deviation in the grand scheme of things was Kalyani. However, eventually, that too fizzled out. But this girl, Priya, looked like a bright piece of cloud shining in the sun. No, not even Priya.

For a moment, Nirmal felt as if it was not Priya. The girl wearing a pair of glittering blue sapphire earrings was not Priya but Kalyani. The scent of unfamiliar flowers, the allure of untold tales, the gleaming eyes of a stranger, and the enigmatic Kalyani.

Kalyani's yelling had lingered on for a long time. 'Just with this strength? Just for this… Only for this much?'

Padmavat keeps thinking. After many years he aspires to defeat Kalyani. He wants to humiliate her. Kalyani, who now slumbers in Park Street Cemetery. He turns eccentric but conceals his emotions. He remains pensive and melancholic. Silence is his veil.

It dawned on Nirmal that it was Priya who stood before him; he was reminded of the fact that Kalyani had been resting in Park Street Cemetery for the past eleven years. Yet, he could see Kalyani in Priya. Their resemblance could not be ignored. The same scent, the same rhythm, similar glow, the same romance and, alone in the cacophonous and crowded intersection of a big city, just like a deer that has been set free. But it was not Priya, it felt like Kalyani.

The notion unnerved him. How did these mortal illusions, these grim existential illusions germinate in his mind? He yearned to rid himself of these hallucinations.

Upon closing his eyes, all the visions vanished. The room appeared blurry and indistinct to him. Nirmal looked awfully ugly and old. But when Priya asked again, he said, 'I'll take you there whenever you want to go. Kalyani Mansion is your home too. It was my desire that your father would come and stay there and open a nursing home. But he didn't budge and ignored my proposal outright.'

The initial sip of coffee itself induced a coughing fit in Dr Raghuvansh. The coffee was exceptionally strong, likely lacking milk. Tears filled his eyes as the cough intensified, and he found himself struggling for breath. In the midst of it, the cigarette butt slipped from his hand, landing on the mosaic floor. Nirmal promptly crushed it beneath his shoe—a useless piece of cigarette and an unwarranted spark of fire.

'Nirmal Bhai, bring Bhabiji home someday. I have seen her pictures in society magazines. Please introduce me to her. We are doing a variety show for our college library. We'll be honoured if Mrs Padmavat inaugurates it.' Priya smiled, and Nirmal Padmavat attempted to pretend he didn't notice. It suddenly struck him that Shirin must have been waiting for him. That she must be lying on the edge of the rectangular Ganga–Jamuni bed in a straight-angle posture, like a thick wreath of *bela* flowers. A bottle of vermouth on the side table... Shirin sips the vermouth sporadically from a tiny blue glass. She presses the bolster between her thighs, smiles and shudders, with her eyes closed. She stares at the ceiling. A massive chandelier made of both white and coloured glass swings from the middle of the ceiling. A strong breeze passes through the open windows and collides with the lampshades of the chandelier. This interaction creates a gentle melody—subtle waves of the water and delicate sounds reverberating against the mirrors—and the soft sounds are utterly tranquillizing.

Shirin gazes at the wall before her. Half the wall is adorned with a huge painting, depicting the side view of a hill station. Hand-pulled rickshaws laden with men, while Tibetan women throng the sides of roads in their gemstone and brass jewellery shops. The snow-clad mountain tops, children running on snow—there is a hill station in the background. There are two women in the foreground, one woman is very fair, and the other is dark-complexioned. Both are standing, leaning on to the railings at the side of the roads, staring at each other with a lot of longing and desire. They are oblivious to the snow-clad mountains, or the children playing on the roads. They are unmoved by the beauty and the change of weather or the deep gorge. Their focus is solely on each other, their glances revealing affection but also a fierce intensity in their eyes that are devoid of serenity.

Shirin gazes at the glowing warmth, savouring the vermouth. Unlike rum, which causes intoxication by swiftly coursing from the throat to the chest and then to the brain, this alcohol demands to be savoured. It permeates each part of the body gradually, offering a sweet effect. Shirin has a fondness for sweetness. While she enjoys warmth, she has no desire to burn or melt like a volcano. Instead, she longs to smoulder slowly, akin to charcoal.

Shirin lives on the twenty-ninth floor of Kalyani Mansion. Her flat has a total of seven rooms. And whenever she wants, she communicates via telephone and comes to the rooftop flat on the thirtieth floor. She comes over to Nirmal's flat, but never does she barge into his bedroom without informing him. Nirmal had once forbidden her to do so. He rarely calls for Shirin. Even when summoned, there are times when she prefers not to ascend the stairs. She enjoys reclining on the peacock bed, gazing at the expansive painting on the opposite wall. However, if Nirmal Padmavat calls for her, she has no alternative but to comply.

Nirmal said, 'Doctor, I have visited you for a specific reason. Tomorrow, we are celebrating Shirin's birthday at Citizens' Club. Priya and you will have to grace the occasion with your presence. It's been two years since our wedding, and yet, you have not met Shirin. She wants to meet you.'

'Why Citizens' Club? You could have invited guests to your residence?' asked Doctor Raghuvansh.

Padmavat understood the meaning of the question. Shirin's ex-husband Vishwajeet Mehta, alias Vishu Mehta, was still the chairman of Citizens' Club. Shirin was Shirin Mehta before getting married to Padmavat. After winning the divorce case at the Presidency Magistrate's Court, she became Padmavat. However, she had already moved in with Nirmal Padmavat six months prior to winning the case. Driving her black Cadillac, she had left the mammoth gate of Southern Avenue's Mehta House. Mehta Sahab stood quietly on the balcony, waiting for Shirin to turn back and look at him for once. She didn't. Vishwajeet Mehta knew deep within that she had left forever, never to return. But he didn't know that she was going to Nirmal Padmavat.

Nirmal had insulted him, but Mehta couldn't avenge this insult. He was capable of taking revenge, but he was scared. Padmavat is not a human being but a frightful monster. He is not a human, rather he's the great poet Goethe's Mephisto, Shakespeare's Othello, Emily Brontë's Heathcliff. This man is the devil.

Unable to endure her husband's insults, Shirin Mehta went straight to Nirmal Padmavat. Disregarding the liftman's refusal, she boarded the elevator at Kalyani Mansion, ascending to the rooftop flat on the thirtieth floor. But she became terrified after reaching the terrace. The long roof of Kalyani Mansion seemed to be asleep like the sleeping sea in the darkness of the night. No sound, no words, no echo. Only deathly silence.

Nirmal's flat was constructed on one side. Adjacent to the doorframe, a pair of Alsatian dogs were tethered with sturdy iron chains. Strangely, they didn't give a bark at the sight of Shirin. Both dogs sat in silence. The thick glass on the steel windows revealed a faint light from inside; no other details were discernible. The windows and doors were shut.

It was eight o'clock at night, and the liftman had already descended with the elevator. But not before saying in a complaining tone, 'Today I'll lose my job, Memsahib. For, I brought you upstairs without the knowledge and permission of my master.'

Shirin Mehta was petrified of this engulfing silence on the terrace. She ran towards the other side of the terrace, as if she wanted to touch and see its length. The terrace was so huge that a stadium could easily be built for a football match.

Shirin walked towards the corner of the terrace, leaned against the waist-high ledge and peered down. As a man ascends, the desire to forget the ground below grows, driven by a fear that emerges in him when he glances downwards— the intrinsic fear of falling. However, Shirin Mehta, standing on the thirtieth floor, decided to peek down anyway, and all her fears suddenly dissipated. She realized what all sprawled out beneath her across a vast expanse, beautifully illuminated. She spotted Mehta House below and saw Vishu Mehta waiting for her on the balcony while taking a stroll.

Shirin despises waiting. She has no patience for it. Whatever she desires, she wants it at once. Her desires fizzle out when the moment is gone, leaving only a sense of resentment behind.

She gazed up at the sky. Not a single cloud adorned it,

only a few tiny twinkling stars. Shirin sensed the moon was not far away. The wind had transformed into a powerful gale. She contemplated that the moon could be seized with just a slight leap. However, there was no moon in sight. The night was exceptionally dark. *Would the moon not rise tonight?*

The liftman went downstairs and told the private secretary, Dhanwantlal, who immediately telephoned Nirmal. 'A woman went upstairs, disregarding the liftman's attempt to stop her. She pushed him aside and took control of the elevator. The liftman lacked the courage to confront her. She appeared to be from an affluent background, possibly under the influence of alcohol. If instructed, I could dispatch the doorman upstairs...'

Without showing any signs of panic, Nirmal told Dhanwantlal, 'Leave it. It must be Shirin Mehta. The wife of the owner of Mehta Industries. You inform Vishu Mehta that Shirin has come here. He should not be worried about her. I'll pacify her and send her back.' Afterwards, he immersed himself in reviewing his company's balance sheet. The audit accounts had been finalized, and it was crucial to conduct a final check to ensure there were no discrepancies.

After going through the balance sheet a few times, Nirmal kept the papers safely in a drawer. Stretching his tired limbs, he rose, removed the overcoat from the arm of the chair, and put it on. With his stick in hand, he stepped outside.

Shirin Mehta was standing at the corner of the terrace, enveloped in a web of fog that seemed to engulf her completely.

Nirmal Padmavat was standing in front of his cottage built in a corner, looking at Shirin, who was immersed in the darkness. Both dogs were now alert. Tethered by leashes, they remain calm. However, once set free, they could turn into frenzied creatures. No longer resembling pets, they transform into fierce, wild beasts unafraid of anyone except Nirmal Padmavat, whom they held in fear.

The woman standing on the far side of the terrace is not Shirin Mehta but Kalyani. Not Shirin but Kalyani. This was a dream embedded in his heart like an arrow since his childhood. If the arrow is pulled out, life will also come out with it. Kalyani had mentioned to Nirmal while standing on the porch of Shangri-La Hotel, 'Only till here! You cannot go beyond this point. Only cars can go beyond this, or high-rise buildings, or bank accounts, or even golden bricks and pieces of diamonds, but not Nirmal Padmavat! This is Kalyani's flat. It is not a brothel of Manhattan's Black women.'

Nirmal had returned and he never went back again. He remained silent, concealing his dreams behind the last beats of his heart. He walked alone, quietly, on the crowded roads. A ten-eleven-year-old, dark-skinned, hideous and frail boy whose mother sold their house and eloped with a lorry driver, leaving him all alone.

This boy was a stranger to the world of banks, civilizations, companies, cultures, income tax, republic, religion and the factories that incessantly emitted poisonous smoke. A stranger, akin to an elephant cub, was being hauled out from a circus. A stranger, similar to someone who came from the mountains of Nepal, perhaps a Gorkhali youth working in the circus, who joined the Gorkha platoon. His offspring balances himself on all fours on the three-legged stool out of fear of the ringmaster's whip, raises his trunk and salutes the spectators.

A Gorkhali young man carries a rifle on his shoulder for bread, wine and his blind mother who must be sobbing and waiting for him in the mountains. In Germany, or in France, or in Korea, or in Japan, in a bombing, or in a guerrilla warfare, or in a field, or in a hospital, he is killed. An article in the military gazette will read, 'Lance Naik Ranbahadur Thapa or Havaldar Khadagmansingh, Gorkha Rifles, number three thousand seven hundred and eighteen or four thousand one hundred and twenty-two, died while fighting on the Imphal or Kashmir or Léopoldville or Amsterdam front.' No one in the mountains, where Ranbahadur Thapa or Khadagmansingh's mother lives, reads the military gazette. Who can recall from which jungle the baby elephant was forcibly taken? No one remembers who died. No one remembers or acknowledges who dies a thousand deaths every single day. Nobody remembers this. People continue to die, just like that. Those who don't know how to perpetuate their life and leave evidence of their existence are forgotten. What's the benefit of remembering? Who is lost in this arduous journey, who is wandering to which destination, and why should one be remembered? The procession will persist. People will keep joining, walk together and inevitably be left behind.

Nirmal Padmavat did not step on the three-legged stool. He did not place a rifle on his shoulder, nor did he greet the spectators. He did not join the procession. He did not die. Instead, he lived. He gave proof of his life, although he *was* a stranger. He chose the illuminated path for himself— illuminated with money and profits. However, there was an arrow in his heart. The arrow was not pulled out because it was a dream and not a wound. The one who has the strength in his soul to keep his dreams alive does not die. Thus, Nirmal did not die, nor did Shirin Mehta.

Shirin was drowning in the web of darkness and fog. Nirmal

kept standing in front of his cottage. The Alsatian dogs were desperate to be unleashed from their chains.

Shirin then looked at Nirmal Padmavat, quietly, but didn't come close. She waited. Nirmal strode towards her. With the help of his stick, he crossed the long distance on the roof to go towards her.

Shirin smiled. Nirmal Padmavat was habituated to such archetypal smiles. The receptionists at big offices smiled like this. The brokers who sell shares of new companies also smiled like this. The hotel managers, the theatre artists, actors, political leaders, everyone smiles like this. But there is only one smile that he liked—a saccharine-drenched smile.

Nirmal didn't ask why Shirin had come there like a maniac, without asking for permission from anyone. He didn't question her; instead, he said, 'When you have come this far, you could have come inside the flat. Why are you standing outside? Let's go inside and sit. I was waiting for you. I thought you would call me, you would come over. But anyway, come inside.'

Nirmal Padmavat reached out and held both of Shirin's hands. But Shirin yelled, 'Leave my hands. I'll walk on my own.'

Nirmal's hands were like iron handcuffs, sending a tingling sensation through Shirin. *Can a man be as hard as a rock? Not a man. Nirmal is not a man.* Shirin stood there, caressing her wrists, and smiling… *What now?*

'I have informed Mehta that you are here. Come, Shirin, and sit in the room. You must be tired. You look agitated. What's the matter? Are you angry with me? But why?' Nirmal clicked the lighter, intending to dispel the darkness. He wanted to smoke.

'I am not agitated. I have come here after much deliberation. I wanted to see you up close. I wanted to see the man who could insult someone like Vishu Mehta. I have no other business here.' Shirin slowly advanced towards the cottage, walking at a distance from Nirmal, carefully weighing every step.

The Alsatians bowed their heads.

Business information from the teleprinter was strewn across the vast table in the massive room. The day's posts, trunk call messages, crucial official files, the latest newspapers—everything lay scattered. Apart from these things, Dhanwantlal, his secretary, had placed a birthday card and a handful of fresh black roses on the table.

It was Nirmal's birthday that day. He had turned forty that year and had forgotten about it. The black roses reminded him of his age. He had met Kalyani for the last time on this very day nineteen years ago. That day too was his birthday, and he had visited Kalyani's apartment. Kalyani had looked like a marble carving of Aphrodite—the naked image of beauty. This day Shirin was looking the same. Similar features, same age, same fickleness, the same smile. Also, the same laziness in the eyes, same fragrance, same rhythm, same spark, the same wild echo of Gypsy music.

It is not Shirin Mehta, it is Kalyani.

Kalyani picked up the cigarette case and matchbox from the table and sat on the sofa, swaying her legs. Her hands were placed on her knees, and a cigarette was hanging from the corner of her lips. She had long eyelashes, the long fingers of an artist. Nirmal's broad shadow is spread across the front wall, appearing shorter than his length.

There was no clock in the room, not even a watch on Nirmal's wrist. Shirin's wristwatch had stopped working. If the watch is not manually winded every day, it stops working. Winding is essential for the watch to work properly.

Punctuality is essential to know time, to understand the essence of time. What's the time now? Time for what and why?

It is not Kalyani, it is Shirin Mehta.

Nirmal kept the greeting card in the drawer. While reviewing the balance sheet of his company, he did not notice the flowers or the greeting card. The balance sheet devoured all his time and focus. He had to read some important papers and letters. He also had to read his secretary's daily reports. National Jute Mill's trade union had written a warning letter yet again. They were to go on a strike from the next week.

Kalyani Mansion Workers Committee's chairman had been wanting to meet him since a few days. The employees had been demanding a hike in their salary. Dearness allowance needed to be given to them. Dhanwantlal had written, 'There is a requirement for cement and iron permits for the new jute mill. The Minister of Control Department will have to be given a party at some grand hotel.' Nirmal smiled after reading about throwing a party. He doesn't resort to offering bribes, be it in the form of money, an escort's companionship, a lavish liquor party in upscale hotels or a musical gathering over drinks. He will not offer bribes. None of this matters much to him. Cement and iron are not a big deal, neither is the jute mill, nor Kalyani Mansion. Nothing holds significant importance for him.

Nirmal doesn't offer bribes. He makes deals. He purchases and sells. Neither is he interested in the intermediate profits nor does he allow others to reap these profits. He despises brokerage. He pays the money to the person from whom he buys the goods. And he takes money from the person to whom he sells the goods. There are no intermediaries or middlemen in his dealings.

He would not throw a party for the control minister

standing between the cement factory and the jute mill. And why on earth does he need to throw him a party? Nirmal requires cement, and the cement factory needs money for its raw materials. Then who is this control minister? Has he made the cement? Has he constructed the factory? The party will be given to the owner of the cement factory on account of the jute mill because the former will give sacks of cement to Nirmal. Thousands of sacks. And what will the control minister give? Just a permit on a piece of paper!

What is the price of this permit? Nirmal Padmavat despises permits. Last night, Vishwajeet Mehta, the owner of Mehta Industries, wanted to give a permit to Nirmal. Permit to join the Citizens' Club, the permit to go on the dance floor with Shirin Mehta, and the permit to dance to the tune of a waltz's heady music.

In ordinary situations, Nirmal Padmavat wouldn't indulge in clubs and society gatherings. Whatever he is, he is not a democrat. He doesn't know how to lie smoothly. He doesn't know tales of hunting and trade and love. He is not talkative. And he is a teetotaller. He doesn't play cards—bridge or rummy—nor does he play billiards. He doesn't play with the wives of his friends. In fact, he doesn't have friends.

He only has one friend, Dr Raghuvansh, who is eternally engrossed in his hospital, laboratory or nursing home. Nirmal doesn't have any other friends, nor does he need anyone else, for he is just like a machine—always running, without a halt. But Mr Mathur, the chief engineer of Thompson Shipping Company had said to him yesterday, 'Today you must come with me to Citizens' Club. There's a Monsoon Ball this evening. The crème de la crème of the society will be there. Numerous businessmen desire to meet you. Many of them have persuaded me to bring you along. Please, Nirmal Sahib, consider my request.'

'You carry on, I'll reach there by 11,' Nirmal had said briskly. He had agreed to this request because it had been ages since he had danced. He used to dance with Kalyani on the dance floor of the Shangri-La Hotel. All the dancing duos despised Nirmal, but they couldn't help but be captivated when they saw Nirmal and Kalyani dancing together. The two would look like a black prince and a fairy princess—Nirmal and Kalyani. Many couples were dancing or sitting on the chairs, yet everyone's eyes used to be transfixed on Kalyani and Nirmal. Nirmal's moves were magical, while Kalyani infused her dance with a captivating madness; where Nirmal's legs exhibited magic, Kalyani's exuded a certain savagery.

Waves of music would swirl as feet would synchronize with the rhythm and cadence, moving around, sliding, and riding on the crest of waves. Kalyani would press her lips to Nirmal's ear and say, 'I am tired, Nirmal dear.'

Nirmal had accepted the invitation the day before because he had wanted to relive Kalyani's tiredness. He had wanted to recall Kalyani's madness—Kalyani…Shangri-La Hotel…Park Street Cemetery! The feet of the dancers used to wander back to the same place. The waves of music circle back to the same place. There is no alternative but to return, and with it comes the same sense of helplessness and melancholy. At exactly 11 o'clock, Nirmal Padmavat opened the door of his long car and disembarked. Mathur Sahab was waiting for him on the lawn of the Club. Mathur Sahab and Vishwajeet Mehta, the president of Citizens' Club.

Nirmal was not familiar with Mehta Sahab. But the latter's file was lying in his office, complete with a detailed introduction. Mehta Sahab is the director of eighteen companies. He is a shrewd capitalist. He knows all the legitimate and illegitimate tricks of the trade; he is an expert. Initially, he was the legal advisor for an insurance company and had also practised law. Thereafter, he became the director of the same company. How he became the director has been explained at length in the file in Nirmal's office. At the age of forty-five, Vishwajeet Mehta got married to the daughter of a steel factory owner. The owner of the steel factory died soon after, and his two sons met with a car accident and unfortunately, died on the spot. An insurance company, a steel factory, two jute mills, a shipping company, and several others—Vishwajeet Mehta became the owner of eighteen companies overnight, by sheer play of chance and coincidence. But how did *he* become the owner?

After a few years, he divorced his wife, claiming that she, the mother of his three children, had stayed in a hotel for two weeks with her driver. The driver could not be produced in court. He had disappeared into some dark and dingy corner of the country; how and where no one knew! The waiters of the hotel gave testimony in court, so did the manager. The police produced evidence. Eventually, Vishwajeet Mehta's wife had to leave Mehta House with her children. Mehta is merciful; he sends ₹200 to his wife monthly for his children. The wife's driver's salary too was ₹200.

Before being noticed by Mehta Sahab, Shirin used to sing English songs at a posh restaurant in the city. She used to reside in a rented house with her elder sister. She was around eighteen years old at that time. At that age, it is not considered decent to stand on a dimly lit stage of a restaurant holding a microphone and singing steamy songs. It is not a matter of pride. However, despite all the efforts from her elder sister, Shirin left Senior Cambridge studies and joined an orchestra. Initially, she used to sing in cultural programmes. Eventually, she became a professional.

Patrons from the city's high society frequented the restaurant where she performed in the evenings. Shirin Salzberg gained recognition in the vibrant world of city nightclubs and upscale hotels. Shirin Salzberg…

Shirin's father, Abraham Salzberg, used to live in Israel with his Jewish wife. He was a Christian. He could not survive for long in Israel and returned to India after his wife's death. Thereafter, he also left for the heavenly abode, leaving some money and a loan behind. Salzberg Sahab was a religious man; he was also a painter. Many of his paintings are related to the life of Jesus Christ and have been preserved in the Victoria Memorial Museum. Even now, the elderly residents of the city remember him vaguely. Every evening, he could be seen strolling with his young daughters along the serene footpath of Chowringhee.

Shirin Salzberg used to sing in restaurants during the evenings and would return to her sister long before the restaurants closed. Both prayed together and then, they would close their eyes and sleep in the same bed, huddled under the same quilt. There was no frustration in life, nor humiliation. No trace of loss. Both sisters used to think that they would not marry and instead spend their lives in this rented house. Bathing in the same bathroom, sharing meals from the same plate, sleeping in the same bed— what more does one need to be happy? There was a radio, some clothes, some books too. The clothes that the sisters wore would be of similar design and colour. People thought they were twin sisters. Shirin was four years younger, but she had a round, voluptuous body. She used to look like a Kashmiri woman when she donned saris. Calcutta's hot and sultry weather had affected her ivory complexion. And what affected her the most was the nonchalance, fickleness and pandemonium of city life.

One day, she realized that her elder sister had been returning home very late and had a new-found interest in fashion. Though they slept together in the same bed, she wouldn't snuggle anymore; neither would she shower affection on her, nor was she mad at her. She would just smile all the time. Quite often the landlord's daughter would come over and say, 'Suzie, there's a phone call for you.'

The younger sister was curious to know who was telephoning her elder sister. She was terrified at the thought of her sister getting married and leaving her alone. This fear taught Shirin the importance of being strong, the importance of being able to go about her life all by herself, alone.

Shirin began to sing steamier and more savage songs on the restaurant stage, which started fetching a bigger crowd. Shaking her hair hanging loose about her shoulders, spreading her arms, with a killer smile on her lips and a wild gleam in her eyes, Shirin Salzberg began to sing...

The boys of Calcutta
Oh, Oh
The boys of Calcutta
They really know how to kiss
They know how to...
Oh, Oh
The boys of Calcutta
They know how to net a fish
They really know...

People started to throng the restaurant in large numbers to witness wild songs sung by a wild girl. Seth Tarachand, Khan Bahadur Yusuf Ali, Maharani Shyamgarh, 'Jute Prince' Krishnan Chettiar and Vishwajeet Mehta too were in the crowd.

The day Mehta Sahab entered Shirin's elder sister's room, the same day he called his lawyer and declared, 'The time has arrived. Start preparations for filing a divorce.'

Shirin Mehta was appointed as the director of Mehta Industries even before the wedding. After the wedding, she went to Europe for three years and learnt the rules and ways of a posh life. She learnt everything that was required to be worthy of being Vishwajeet Mehta's wife.

She learned to be a part of high society, and yet, the wildness did not diminish from her eyes. Sometimes the same lowliness starts resurfacing on her face, a look that gets etched on the faces of women who sing in restaurants and sleep on rented beds. Shirin is an ignoble woman whose conduct and behaviour do not have the decency of noble women of feudal families. There is a lack of aristocracy and elegance. Whatever Shirin desires, she demands it outrightly. If she has the power, she snatches it away. Shirin doesn't play chess; instead, she gambles. The infamous teen patti or 3 card brag. If she wins, she is ecstatic, and if she loses, she begins to sob. Later, she forgets and dozes off. She doesn't have any regrets about the past, nor does she worry about the future. The only way left for her is to live in the here and the now. *It was dark before; darkness will befall again. Even if there remains only a sliver of light, then live it up. This single ray is what is life! This ray...this flower...*

That night on the thirtieth floor, pressing her feet together like a clever cat, Shirin Mehta rose. She came and stood beside the table near Nirmal Padmavat. Nirmal was seeing a woman so close to him after many years, and yet, he was not happy. He was marooned in his own thoughts.

Shirin picked up the roses and suddenly happiness enveloped her. She said, 'Uff, these black roses...Nirmal

Babu, I am seeing black roses for the first time (I'm seeing you for the first time)…these flowers are very beautiful, fresh and extremely poisonous (the flowers are just like you)…black tulips, black roses, black…Nirmal Babu, do you believe in destiny or not?'

Nirmal continued to maintain that he did not believe in destiny. He didn't have faith in deeds, nor on religion, or ethics. He didn't even believe in God. For he believed that dependency on deeds made us inert. Morality was nothing but the walls of a false prison. Religion made us blind the moment we believed in God because then we ceased to believe in our own strength.

Morality was an addiction, just like sin. It too was a habit. Morality made a man subjugated and blind, just like the love of a woman turns us blind. Just like the old Julius Caesar was blinded by Cleopatra, whom he perceived as an innocent child. Just like Kalyani, or Shirin Mehta. What was morality but a habit of debauchery?

Why would Nirmal believe in such a habit? Or destiny? He wouldn't even trust Shirin Mehta. He would only take revenge, not from Vishwajeet Mehta, but from the woman sleeping peacefully in the Park Street Cemetery. Vishwajeet Mehta had not harmed him, nor did he have the ability to harm him. He could sneer, ridicule, abuse, pass statements, but couldn't harm. He could only ask repeatedly, 'Dr Raghuvansh's wife also used to live in New York. Did you know her? She used to live in Shangri-La. I've danced with her many times. She was a nice lady! Did you know her? She was very popular among the Indians of New York City.'

Sitting at the cocktail table in the massive hall of the Citizens' Club, Mehta Sahab started asking the same question repeatedly to his guest. Nirmal feigned ignorance and got busy introducing himself to other people. Everyone was eager to meet him. People marvelled at his success, as no man could become the owner of a thirty-storey-high skyscraper in such a short time. *Nirmal Padmavat is like a magician. He secretly imports gold from Arab and Israel; he organizes bank robberies. He makes fake notes. Nirmal Padmavat is a magician, a devil!*

There was a swarm of men and beautiful women on both sides of the long table. The cocktail session was on. Mathur Sahab continued to make introductions. Nirmal was the centre of attraction. That's when Vishwajeet Mehta asked, 'Why did you name your building Kalyani Mansion? Wasn't Kalyani the wife of Dr Raghuvansh?'

'Yes, Kalyani was an acquaintance; and, it is otherwise a beautiful name, more beautiful than Shirin.' Nirmal indulged in light satire with Mehta Sahab for the first time in a long while. Laughter erupted from everyone present. Nirmal was aware that Mehta had to put in a lot of effort to marry Shirin. Moreover, Nirmal knew Shirin's background from before her marriage. Nirmal knew everything. He had files and files on the capitalists and political leaders of the city in his office, which had all the information about their lives. This information has been a massive fortune for Nirmal.

The dance was to commence right after the round of cocktails. The orchestra was to start shortly. People were to pull their chairs to the sides, leaving the floor vacant. Couples were to rise from the chairs to dance to the tunes of the music. The decibel level was going to increase, and so would the pace of dance.

When Nirmal Padmavat took her name, Shirin Mehta was walking with a friend, holding a small glass in her hand. She was welcoming the guests. Suddenly, she turned and said, 'Who took my name? Who has the courage?', and came and stood behind her husband's chair. Mehta Sahab started laughing and said, 'Even if the name is not beautiful, my Shirin is a paragon of beauty, and nobody even comes close to her.'

Shirin was ecstatic to hear this. Nirmal raised his eyes and looked but once at Shirin Mehta, and said, smiling, 'Mr Mehta, I think you haven't even seen a picture of Kalyani. You must pay Dr Raghuvansh a visit and see her picture.'

Shirin was filled with hatred and fury on hearing his remarks. She had spent five hours at a famous salon on Lindsay Street to look the way she did for the Monsoon Ball. All of five hours were spent doing make-up. And now this black man insists on seeing someone else's picture!

There is no other purpose in Shirin Mehta's life except beauty and her efforts to maintain her youth. The long fingers of her hands, the nails, the eyelashes, the fair ankles, the calves, the lips, the arms; she cares for and cossets each and every part of her body. All that's left is to wrap it in cotton wool. She has no other tasks except pampering her body and sometimes lying in Vishwajeet Mehta's bed. By the way, she is the chairperson of many social institutions, director of several companies, and attends society meetings, conducts inaugurations, distributes prizes, caresses the back of her horses at the racecourse, purchases anything and everything she fancies from posh markets. But she is not really keen on any of that as much as grooming and make-up. She is not interested even in going to bed, because the bed is cold. Vishu Mehta has aged. There is no malleability, no flexibility, no tenderness at all in his old age. He has the rigidity of a dried tree.

Shirin pines for greenery. She longs for her elder sister's bed. She yearns for tenderness and love. She used to feel at peace and was contented when sleeping with her head on her elder sister's arm. Now she fears even having to talk to Vishwajeet Mehta. She fears the rigidity, the attack. She fears the dried branches. She doesn't want any of it.

Shirin doesn't want to ever grow old and ugly. She is a proletarian. She has lost everything. Now she wants to hold on to her youth and beauty. In her make-up room, she stands in front of the life-size mirror and stares at herself and admires her form.

It was as if this illusion was shattered by Nirmal's jab. She banged the empty glass on the table and walked away— fuming, burning, writhing in anger.

But it was for an entirely different reason that Mehta Sahab was angry with Nirmal. The land on which Nirmal had built Kalyani Mansion belonged to Mehta Sahab's first wife. While dying, Mehta Sahab's father-in-law had willed this land to his daughter. Being blinded by Shirin's love and with his insane concern about divorcing his first wife as soon as possible, Mehta had forgotten about it; if he hadn't, he would have somehow gotten the land transferred to his name. Anyway, the land was in their possession.

The wife got a divorce. And then Nirmal Padmavat bought the entire land from Mehta Sahab's ex-wife after their divorce. Mehta Sahab ended up filing a case at the civil court, only to lose. He lost in the high court too, unable to retrieve the land by any means. Nirmal eventually laid the foundation of Kalyani Mansion.

That was the real reason for his anger. And it was because of this anger that Vishwajeet Mehta said, 'I do not need to see Kalyani's picture, Mr Padmavat! I used to visit New York City every year during the winter and would stay at the Shangri-La Hotel. I used to call for your Kalyani every night. Fifty dollars. That's all she charged for a night. Fifty dollars and a bottle of vermouth.'

Nirmal Padmavat stood up from his chair like a sword pulled from its sheath. In a very soft tone he said, 'Mehta Sahab, Kalyani is dead. Do not sully her name.'

And as he said this, Nirmal's face turned hideous. Numerous deep lines appeared—dark lines. As if, for a moment, he had morphed into a ferocious beast. But the drunk Vishwajeet Mehta did not look at him. He started yelling at the top of his voice, 'Who am I to sully her name! I am not a pimp. Why would I sully her name? But Kalyani was a prostitute! She…was…a…prostitute. She was not a noblewoman. God only knows how she trapped the doctor! She was—'

Before he could finish his sentence, Nirmal, leaning forward, grabbed his collar with the claws of his right hand and pulled him with all his might, and with his left hand he delivered a powerful blow to his face.

Mehta Sahab screamed, his chair overturned, with him in it, and he fell to the floor unconscious. Blood started oozing out of his mouth.

It was a weird incident for the Citizens' Club. Civilized people from high society fought amongst themselves over their girlfriends by drinking alcohol or gambling. They abused each other but did not resort to scuffles. Fighting was the work of fools, educated people used their intelligence. If not intelligence, then money. But to fight, to cause bloodshed, to murder were considered the ways of hooligans of Macchua Toli, China Town, Wellesley Street. Goons could be bought with money. There was no need to get involved in a scuffle yourself.

People in the room were panic-stricken to see blood oozing out of Mehta Sahab's mouth; he lay senseless on the floor. Women were screaming and fainting. A fat Gujarati gentleman started calling for the police. But Nirmal kept standing in his place, unmoved. Calm, steady and still! That ugliness had disappeared from his face. There was tenderness. His monstrous appearance had diminished. He seemed like a man, a strong and courageous man, who knew how to stand up for himself and take revenge for his insults.

A few waiters took Mehta Sahab to the washroom, and thereafter, he was given first aid. Within half an hour, Mehta Sahab recovered and emerged bashfully. He came directly to Nirmal and said, 'If you harboured so much love for Kalyani, why didn't you marry her?'

Saying this, he started smiling. Nirmal didn't smile back, nor did he say anything. At a distance, near the bandstand, Shirin Mehta stood watching. Nirmal was looking at her.

Shirin Mehta was standing in his flat and Nirmal was looking at her. Whereas, Shirin was gazing at the black roses. She turned to Nirmal and said, 'You don't believe in luck. But I do. It was sheer luck that you went to the Citizens' Club last night, and he teased you about your lover.'

Having said this, Shirin Mehta, placing both her palms on the desk, bent over in front of this dark and ugly ten-year-old ignorant boy, and burst into laughter. She was laughing with all the strength in her chest. She laughed as if this flat of Nirmal would be burnt to ashes in the fire of her laughter. It felt that Kalyani Mansion would collapse like a mound of sand in this earthquake of laughter, and this entire earth would become a volcano, this entire sky would be filled with smoke, strong flames, darkness and death. As if Shirin Mehta...

When Nirmal Padmavat looked up, it was Kalyani who was standing in front of him. The same familiar fragrance of unfamiliar flowers. The same familiar rhythm of unknown songs. The same sympathetic gleam in strangers' eyes. And Kalyani…

Shirin Mehta was wearing a red silk sari. She looked like a goddess. There was a necklace of fake diamonds around her neck.

Shirin said, 'Nirmal dear, I don't despise you. I have started despising Mehta. You insulted him royally, and yet, he came and stood in front of you with a bowed head. And to crown it all, he asked me to dance with you!'

Kalyani said, 'You ran away from my room in Shangri-La, Nirmal, and never returned. You were a coward. You were weak. No one can conquer love without courage. I have come…'

Shirin said, 'I have come because I am not a coward like Mehta. I love a strong man, not a coward.'

Kalyani said, 'You must become daring, Nirmal; love will prostrate at your feet. That's why I have come.'

Nirmal Padmavat could not tolerate that immaculate, catastrophic laughter. He came out of the room silently. Kalyani did not come out. Nor did Shirin Mehta. Her laughter remained confined inside the room.

Why does a man oscillate between being strong and being weak? Where does the strength come from? And the weakness?

While Nirmal was not intimidated by Vishwajeet Mehta, at all, he was petrified of the latter's wife who had visited his flat. Just like he had feared Kalyani. He was terrified and so he ran away. He ran away from his own room. He continued to stroll on the rooftop of his 30-storey building for a long time. Lonely and sad. Sadness had become a way of life for Nirmal—sadness, loneliness, toil and a dream that pierced his heart like an arrow.

He lost track of time. There was darkness all around. Electric lamps were glowing on the streets below. There was no moonlight. Does a man sell his entire past, his whole present, all his achievements, his complete being for this darkness? *For this darkness?* For this deep slumber, in which—even after immersing oneself—a man cannot dream?

Nirmal Padmavat kept wandering in the darkness of the terrace. He didn't even have his stick in his hand. His legs started to ache. His eyes were about to be shut. His throat was parched but there was no water. There was not even a single drop of water in that river of darkness. Not even one drop!

He stood at the corner of the terrace and peeked over. It was so easy to jump from the terrace. It was so easy to be rescued from a bad dream. To pull an arrow out of the chest.

Kalyani, standing at the door of his flat, yelled, 'Nirmal, come back!'

Shirin Mehta, standing at the door of his flat, yelled, 'I am scared of the darkness, Nirmal.'

Nirmal smiled and began to return slowly. Advancing towards the latter, he said, 'Let's go out, Shirin. We'll sit at the banks of the Hooghly for some time, then I'll drop you off at Mehta House.'

'Let's go. But I'm not going back to Mehta House ever. Would you make me go back to him?' Shirin asked and glided towards Nirmal.

It is such a weird question, Nirmal thought. *She is a weird girl indeed.*

Nirmal stood in the lift. Shirin Mehta kept smiling, taking the support of Nirmal's arms. The lift started descending. The liftman was surprised. Who was this woman who went upstairs like a maniac, and now seemed to be in a trance?

He was seeing Nirmal with a woman for the first time. In fact, he was seeing such a beautiful woman for the first time. He was happy with his master's choice. The master understood that. Nirmal asked, 'Fredrick, are you married?'

The liftman was a bit jittery, as it was the first time in years that his master had spoken to him. Playfully, he said, 'Yes, Sir! It's been three years.'

'Do you have kids?' Nirmal smiled.

'Yes, Sir! I have a year-old baby girl, Sir! The month she was born, Manager Sahab increased my salary by twenty rupees, Sir! We are very comfortable, Sir!' Fredrick would have continued to speak but the doors of the lift soon opened. Shirin Mehta and Nirmal walked out of the lift.

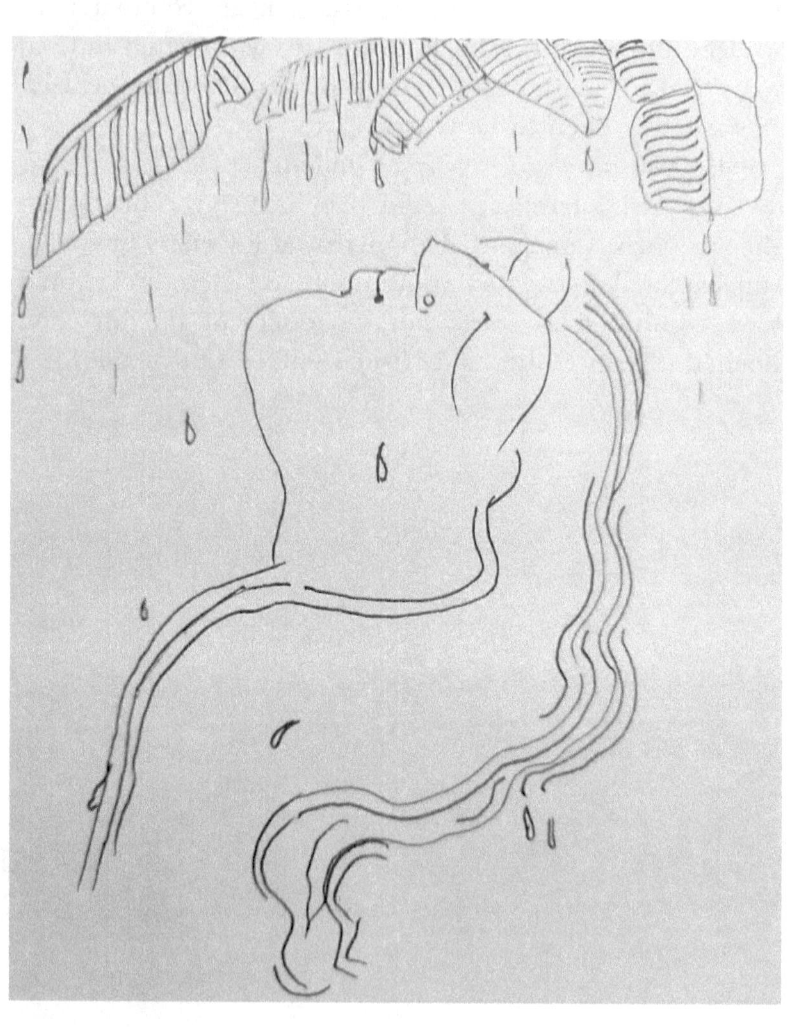

Eight

'Although I didn't want to, Shirin insisted on throwing the party in Citizens' Club. Since it is her birthday, I thought she should decide on the venue herself,' Nirmal told Dr Raghuvansh.

Doctor gave a vapid smile as he abhorred the answer. 'You should have said no to Mrs Padmavat. For I know that Mehta Sahab has become your nemesis. He keeps trying to harm you. But Padmavat...he has the right to do so. You have snatched his wife from him. Do you want to add insult to injury?'

'It is not about insult, Doctor!' Nirmal started saying, 'This is just Shirin's stubbornness—'

'This is not stubbornness, but harshness. Ask your wife to learn to respect—respect not Mehta but you! And if she can't show some respect, she should at least show some compassion. Your wife does not harbour compassion in her heart. If she did, she would not have bailed on her insulted husband.' Dr Raghuvansh said this in a tired tone and started coughing. Priya went to fetch water for him. Nirmal said, 'You are not well. Please take rest. Visit a hill station.'

He feigned ignorance to Nirmal's suggestion and continued, 'The most vital virtue is compassion. Nothing else is important. Only compassion is required. If there is compassion, all our sorrows can be laid aside.' He fell silent after completing his sentence. Priya had arrived with a glass of water in her hand. He drank the water and rose from his chair without uttering a word. He just smiled at Priya—at Nirmal too. Kalyani is so lonely in her grave. As is each one of us in this prison called life. We are ensnared by age, by desires, by dreams, by events of the past and by the uncertainties of the future. Can a thirty-storey skyscraper become our friend? Can medicines become our sympathizers? Injection, operation theatre, patients, different kinds of diseases? Can dance, music and social gatherings be our companions? Can books be our companions?

What truly holds us up are compassion and empathy, kindness and affection. And illusions. But Shirin Padmavat or Nirmal Padmavat do not have these virtues. There is only darkness.

'Well, I'm leaving now. I'll send the invitation card tomorrow morning. Priya, you must bring Doctor along with you.' Saying this, Nirmal started descending the stairs.

Nirmal is a stranger. Nirmal is a stranger to himself.

Nine

Padmavat's secretary Dhanwantlal said to him, 'You must visit the Jute Mill once. The manager is unable to control the situation. He is constantly calling me. The police are there, and yet...'

'But the police demand a bribe, right? First, they demand bribes, then they lathi charge the workers and arrest their leaders. Even trade union people demand bribes. They'll withdraw the strike only upon receiving a bribe. This is what you want to say, right?' Nirmal Padmavat asked this while reviewing the files. There was not even a trace of vexation on his face, or in his mind. He just wondered why all this was happening in the first place.

'Yes, this is exactly how it is!' Dhanwantlal is worried. For he knows that the reason behind the National Jute Mill strike is not the trade union, but Vishwajeet Mehta. He is responsible for all recent happenings. Mehta and his friends have cooked up the ongoing chaos. Mehta Sahab has not forgotten, nor is it possible to forget. This building on Princess Street is very high. Shirin Padmavat travels in a very long and fast car. Nirmal visits the Citizens' Club. He always smiles. Wealthy merchants' and tradesmen's wives drool over him. They are bewitched by him, but he doesn't pay heed to anyone. Nor does he allow anyone to come close to him. He maintains a distance.

'Fine! Ask the manager to close the mill. He should vacate the bungalow and come here.'

'But we have taken many orders for supply. The mill cannot be closed without completing the orders. We would incur a massive loss, and it would be disgraceful for us. The business will be hit.'

'Let it be. We'll bear the loss. But it's not possible for us to offer a bribe.' Nirmal took his final stand and then became silent. He got engrossed in reviewing the files. He was astonished. *Why was this happening?*

He paid his employees the highest wages and the highest bonus. There were decent quarters for the employees. There was a field, a park, a hospital, too. And yet, employees had gone on a strike, giving just a day's notice and halting work. They hold one procession, and just like that, all work is at a standstill. Even the police can't seem to do anything about it. The government keeps mum. The chimneys of National Jute Mill have stopped spewing smoke. Who was the real culprit?

It wasn't the employees' fault, for they were following the orders of their leaders. It wasn't the fault of the union leaders, for they acted in the interest of the employees— as an outcome of the strike, the wages of workers would increase, and they will be offered more amenities. The strike called by the workers union of the National Jute Mill was successful because the owner did not keep the police by his side by paying them bribes. The owner was naïve. He didn't know the workings of this city.

This city runs on bribes. For everything, a bribe must be offered, in the form of money, in the form of gifts or in the form of sweet talk. Nirmal does not know the art of flattery. Nirmal knows hard work, diligence, honesty. He knows that there is no need to know anything else.

Dhanwantlal walked out. And ascending one floor by the stairs, Shirin came to the flat and stood beside Padmavat. 'Give me a minute,' Nirmal said.

At the very moment, Prabhaschandra Niyogi called. 'I have decided. The mill will remain closed until the strike is called off,' Nirmal announced.

'This is a wrong decision. You must agree to all the demands of the employees for now. You should visit personally and assure them that you will appoint a new manager and make new living quarters for new workers. These are their only demands. Thereafter, slowly induct your men into the mill's union. Drive out all the rogue leaders gradually.' Seth Niyogi wanted to show the right path to Nirmal Padmavat. All mill owners act the same way. If you don't work diplomatically, not even a single mill will function. All the factories would cease to exist.

But Nirmal is not diplomatic. He blurted out, ' I can't do all this. Let's get the mill closed. The loss is not mine alone. The workers will not get work anywhere. All the mills are closing down slowly.'

Shirin Padmavat said, 'I'm going out with Priya. We'll go to Diamond Harbor. Shall I go?'

Nirmal forgets everything at the mere mention of Priya's name. Either he forgets, or he wants to forget. Priya and Dr Raghuvansh. Dr Raghuvansh and Kalyani. Everything is connected with a fine thread.

'Where is Priya?'

'She is in her bungalow. She had telephoned me. Can I go?'

'No!' Nirmal raised his head to meet Shirin's gaze. Shirin was becoming restless; she wanted to leave. It was already evening and she wanted to run away. She would return late at night and would sleep quietly in her room while Nirmal would stay awake in his room.

'Do I have to go someplace with you now? Where do you want to go?' Shirin asked in an utterly cold tone.

'You sit in your room, I'll come in a while. We are not going anywhere today.'

Shirin understood that Nirmal was exasperated. Had he not been, he would have agreed to her request. He was outraged. He only goes to Shirin's flat when he is angry. Otherwise, he prefers to stay in his own flat or go out somewhere. He plays rummy in the club, makes business plans, converses with the manager. Or else, he dawdles alone in his Oldsmobile car. He doesn't go to Shirin.

Shirin is then left alone. She telephones Priya and calls her over. Then, she asks her to come very close to her.

She had met Priya for the first time in Citizens' Club on her birthday last year.

Dr Raghuvansh had not turned up that day but Priya was there. Nirmal had introduced them to each other and vamoosed to Mehta Sahab's table straight away. Shirin had recognized Priya and sensed from the very first meeting that they could be friends. That night, by mistake, Shirin had spilt coffee on Priya's clothes. She yelped, 'Let's wash it, otherwise it will stain your sari.'

The coffee stain on the white handloom sari looked very pronounced. Both the women rose immediately and advanced towards the washroom. On the way, Priya said, 'I have come here just to meet with you.'

'The stain will go away if you wash it immediately. Don't worry at all,' Shirin replied.

Priya stood near the washbasin. Shirin soaked the stained end of her sari in water, added soap and started rubbing it. She then squeezed it to strain the excess water out. She said, 'Not to worry now as it will dry quickly.'

Priya gave a subtle smile, but thought, *Why is Shirin so worried? So what if the stain doesn't go away?* Priya smiled again. There is a reflection of Priya in the mirror placed above the washbasin. And Shirin Padmavat is standing right behind her. Two women within a single mirror frame.

Shirin suddenly held Priya in her arms, and said hesitantly, 'Priya, you are very beautiful.'

Nirmal had never said such a thing to Shirin. Perhaps he had never paid attention to her beauty. He had married Shirin just to humiliate Vishwajeet Mehta and to set foot in the high society of rich people. That's it! Perhaps he never tried to witness the radiant beauty of his wife, not even at his leisure.

There is something strange and striking in Shirin's face and her entire body. Sometimes she looks like a paragon of beauty, and at other times, awfully ugly. She never remains in the 'in-between' state at any moment. She is either as hot as a burning desert or as cold as an ice-cold rock. Shirin never remains normal and calm.

Nirmal cannot bear to see this peculiarity of his wife's body. Not even at his leisure. When she came to seek permission to go out with Priya, she was really warm then. Warm, fresh and soft. Soft and very beautiful. But as soon as Nirmal forbade her, she transformed into a shapeless and ugly rock of ice.

Having turned into a rock, she did not wait even for a moment near Nirmal Padmavat. She quietly sneaked out of the room. She didn't enter the lift but, descending the stairs, she returned to her flat. She then telephoned Priya.

'I won't be able to come, Priya! Nirmal is coming to my room.'

'At this time? Doesn't he have any other work? It's just evening...' Priya smirked.

'Why don't you come here, Priya? My life will be spared. If you come, all three of us can go out somewhere.'

'What benefit will I get by saving your life? Nirmal will get mad at me. Call me when you are free, Shirin. I will come over.'

Shirin hung up the phone. The maid was called to arrange the living room and the bedroom. Nirmal was coming to her flat after almost a month. He visits her occasionally, especially when he is vexed. He doesn't need to visit her when he is drenched in love. When he is happy, he keeps his distance from Shirin. When he is happy, he allows Shirin to spend time with Priya.

And Shirin does not wait for his anger, for she is terrified of his temperament. She never wants to see him angry. Nirmal's wrath hurts her a lot. She feels as if Nirmal is pushing her into a dark cave—the dark cave of death. There are poisonous animals in the cave. There are numerous snakes and she has been turned into a fish that has been pulled out of the sea. A blue fish. An unconscious fish. A fish thirsting for water. But the cave is dark. There are numerous snakes in the cave. Poisonous snakes. There is no ray of light left anywhere.

Why does Shirin feel like this? Is it because she is some thirty-thirty-two years old already, and neither Vishwajeet Mehta nor Nirmal Padmavat has given her the gift of motherhood? Is it because of that?

No, Shirin does not want to become a mother. The desire for motherhood had died within her when she was merely a child.

She was five or six years old when her mother was pregnant. She vividly remembers Maa writhing on the bed. There was a midwife standing beside her, a nurse too. Even her father was standing next to her. Maa became unconscious due to excruciating pain. Hours flew by! Maa would calm down sporadically and again would yell and whimper with unbearable pain. At that moment, the midwife and the nurse had dismissed Shirin from the room. Her father also came out, closing the door behind them.

They could hear Maa wailing and yelling in pain. All of a sudden, everything fell quiet. A dead child was taken out of Maa's womb by the midwife's skilled hands. A dead child, dry as wood, turning blue.

Doctors were called for, but unfortunately, Maa could not be saved. Her limbs had swollen. Septicaemia had started spreading throughout her body and she went into septic shock. Maa was dead. Shirin's desire to become a mother had fizzled out at that moment, at the tender age of six.

Her elder sister had secretly told her that a baby came into their Maa's womb only because she had slept beside their father. Maa had become ill because of the conception and had died.

Shirin began to despise her father. She began to loathe not only her father but all men in the world. She only loved her elder sister, and gradually, she began to love all the women around her. Never loved a man. Never, ever.

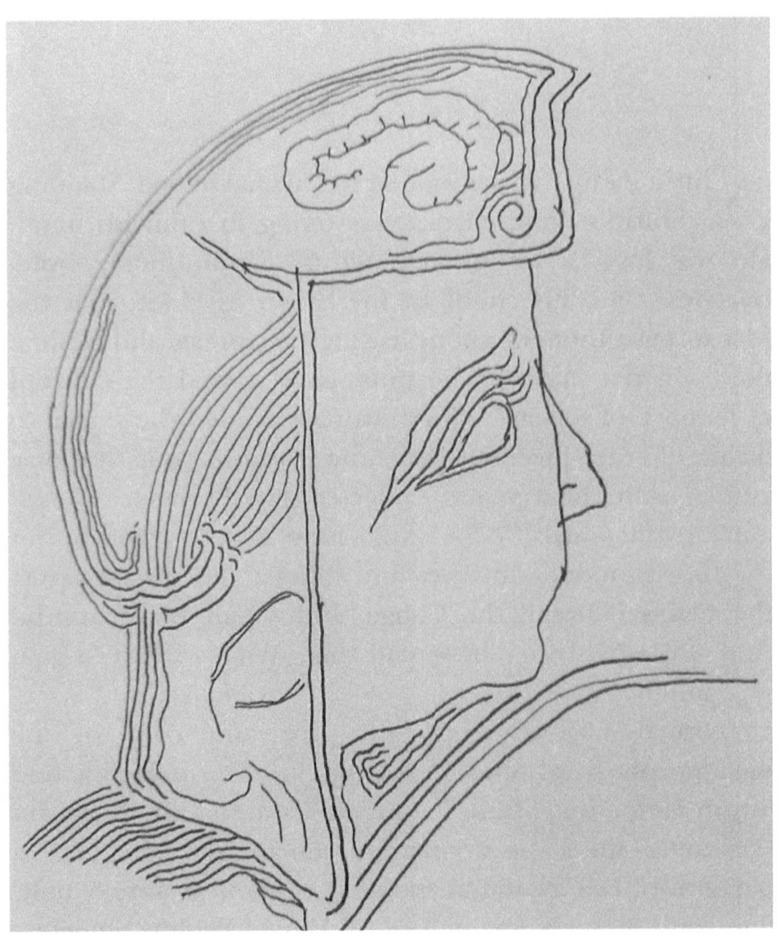

Ten

Shirin Padmavat was waiting for Nirmal in bed. Standing at Shirin's door, Nirmal was trying to calm his mind. He was lost in his own thoughts. Family, home, wife, relatives, clan, his child! In the Stone Age, who was the first to have thought about leaving the forests and settling down on flat plains? Who must have started the concept of family and society? Who must have coined the slogan to divide life into pieces? Divide into portions your weapons, animal skin, quarry and collected wood, divide women among individuals? Who would have said to come out of the forests, mountain caves and valleys; and spread across the plains between the Ganga, Indus and Brahmaputra! And why would they have said that? What's there to gain in a family?

Nirmal was weighing the pros and cons of the metamorphosis of Shirin Salzberg into Shirin Mehta, and Shirin Mehta into Shirin Padmavat. Wouldn't Shirin remain the same—the same woman? A woman who is at once a paragon of beauty and at the next moment is awfully ugly! Someone insanely terrified of all things mighty. Someone intimidated by religion, by the love of a man, by the social system. She wanted to stay concealed, to not come out into the open.

What would Nirmal do with a woman like this? In fact,

what would he do with himself? Kalyani's scream and sob had lingered for long in his psyche.

It dawned on Nirmal that it was he who had dreamed about a family. It was he who had made the accumulation of wealth the basis of family welfare. It was all his doing. It is only me who has made my wife, children, cattle, liquor, meat, deerskin, horse, iron and stone weapons into my personal property. It was my intense affection for material objects and situations that first established our family back in the *Aadi Yug*. I engaged in agricultural work. I went into business, service, sacrifice, education, begging and politics. I started writing history. I made the woman of my choice the mistress of my family. I have procreated…no, no…as if a blazing flame of fire flared up in Nirmal Padmavat's chest. I did not bring a child into this world. I remained childless.

'Why are you standing outside?' This tiny question of Shirin pulled him in. There was a dim light in the room, a shade of blue, similar to the orphaned sky without the stars. There was just the moon, akin to a round piece of ice. And that moon was none other than Shirin. A cold bauble of ice.

Shirin got up from the bed, searching for the sandal of the other foot. A naked black lady is standing on a high tripod stool in one corner, hands clasped, laughing. Her face is dark. Narrow waist, blood-red eyes, red lips, dark arms in some wild dance pose. She is not trying to hide the remnants of nudity by crossing her legs.

This statue dominated everything else in the room. It dominated the books, the flowers, the fluttering curtains, the sofa set, the bed, everything—a naked, black woman, all of two feet in height. Blood-red eyes, crimson lips.

The red lips uttered, 'Are you mad at me? Why didn't you allow me to go out with Priya?'

Nirmal was not looking at Shirin, his gaze was transfixed on the black woman. Kalyani, Priya, Shirin! This Black Lady living inside all three women was driving Nirmal insane. But Nirmal Padmavat was not insane, rather he was very sharp. He cannot be compared with normal people. He takes each step mindfully and never retreats. He always forges ahead. Nirmal had travelled from a small village on a riverbank to Karachi, from Karachi to Bombay, from Bombay to New York, and thereafter, from New York to Calcutta. He thought about his remarkable achievements, starting from the thirty-storey skyscraper, the National Jute Mill, Miller & Miller Co., India Shipping Corporation, West Bengal Bank to Hooghly Glass Works, and to crown it all, Shirin Padmavat.

But why does even a man of this stature turn fragile, vulnerable and insane at some juncture in life?

Gradually age catches up, but the heat doesn't fizzle out. Rather, desires become firmer, and the mind even crazier.

'Sometimes even I need you. What's the big deal if you could not go out with her for one day?' Nirmal asked while moving to the corner and standing in front of the Black Lady. Shirin was annoyed by the dryness in Nirmal's tone. *If this man cannot do anything else, at least he can talk softly.* She replied with disgust, 'Everything will happen according to your whim and fancy, I'm a mere stone.'

Nirmal turned back as if he had been hit by that stone. Shirin stood near the bed, alone, helpless, still looking like a paragon of beauty. A beauty cloaked with hope.

A hungry tiger writhes with profound cravings when it looks at its prey. Suddenly, seeing a loaded rifle pointed at it, a thirsty deer near a water body looks towards the dark shrubs with profound cravings. The forest is silent, wind inert. There is no sound, no movement, not even a ray of light anywhere.

Nirmal Padmavat embraced Shirin. After all, Shirin was his wife, and he had a right to play with her body. He has all kinds of rights—religious rights, social rights, ethical rights. Shirin cannot refuse his advances even if she wants to. Nirmal's arms were rock-solid and his chest, just like a cliff of iron.

Shirin closed her eyes and surrendered to him. Time was like a fast-flowing river, and she wanted to drown in it. Nirmal placed her on his lap and started unbuttoning her blouse. Buttons were on the back of the blouse, and Nirmal's fingers began to quiver while stripping her. Shirin breathed heavily. Her rapid and warm breaths punctured the silence of the room. Nirmal uttered in a trembling voice, 'Today you won't despise me. Not today...'

'Please lock the door...perhaps—' uttering these words, Shirin placed her arms around Nirmal's neck. Nirmal couldn't hear her voice, couldn't comprehend her words. The iron smouldered in the hot electric hearth. Shirin was turning insane with desire. Time seemed to freeze. Shirin had drowned. She had drowned in the hot river of molten iron.

Nirmal was like a hungry tiger, and he sharply gazed at Shirin with his starving eyes. But now Shirin prostrates on the bed; she lay there like a lifeless, soft lump of meat. There were no scars, or inkblots. There was no darkness, nor filth anywhere. Shirin was an impeccable embodiment of physical beauty. And Nirmal Padmavat was going mad, fighting his moral authority.

Nirmal got up from the bed. He removed his clothes and draped them on the hanger. He removed his briefs too but didn't remove his vest. Shirin Padmavat opened her eyes at this point. Almost groaning at the top of her lungs, she blurted, 'Why don't you come here? What is taking you so long? Come here!'

On hearing her squeals, Nirmal felt as if his throbbing nerves would burst, and his body would break into pieces. But before he could disintegrate into pieces, he dove onto Shirin's bed. Shirin was lying face down on the bed. She was quiet. Her eyes were shut. She is a religious woman. Perhaps she is praying.

Shirin is praying to her Almighty that whatever had happened in the past must not be repeated. Not again, for this one time at least! She is praying with all her heart.

Nirmal used the strength of both his hands to drag her towards himself…her eyes were shut, so was her heart. A closed body burns. Red lips burn too. Shirin burned like a hot furnace…but all of a sudden, Nirmal Padmavat felt that the woman lying face down was not Shirin…but Kalyani… Kalyani of Shangri-La Hotel was screaming madly and trying to say something.

It was already too late. Shirin opened her eyes, and extending her hand, tried to get a hold of Nirmal. She yearned to drink him in. But it was already too late. The piece of ice had now melted into water, and it did not take long for water to turn into steam and evaporate into thin air.

When a man loses his manhood, he is like a melting ice cube—he dies. Nirmal is dead.

This is a normal scenario. This happens every time. Nirmal does not take advantage of his moral rights. He is poor—a proletariat.

At this point, Shirin Padmavat leapt out like a fish after tearing the net and dove onto Nirmal's scattered, broken body. She began to beat Nirmal's body with both her hands. 'That was it! This was all you needed? Tell me! You don't care about me at all! Why don't you kill me?'

Suddenly, Priya came in, sliding the curtain, saying, 'Who are you yelling at in the dark, Shirin? Who is here?'

Discovering Nirmal, and then Shirin lying on top of Nirmal, Priya morphed into a statue of stone, similar to Ahalya who was cursed by her husband to become a stone. She froze completely. She couldn't advance any further, neither could she retreat. This was the first time she had seen something like this in real life, although she must have seen it in pictures.

Nirmal Padmavat held Shirin's waist and lifted her with a jerk and threw her ruthlessly on the sofa, just as porters throw parcels in the carriages of a goods train. Shirin lay like a corpse, with half of her body on the sofa and the other half on the floor. She failed to even twist and turn.

Priya quickly rushed to the sofa to help Shirin. Nirmal began to clean his body with a towel, put on his clothes, and walked out of the room. He did not even turn back to look at Priya and Shirin.

'Get up, Shirin, come to the bed. You need rest; forget what has happened,' Priya said.

But Nirmal Padmavat immediately came back. However, he did not enter the room. Standing outside, he asked Priya to come out.

But Priya did not budge. She was beginning to despise Nirmal and feared him. Shirin had told her everything.

Nirmal was sick. He was weak. He didn't know how to hold back. He should rather consult a good doctor before making any advances. But he doesn't go to visit a doctor. Although he was not impotent, he was sick. He was weak. Shirin had revealed everything to Priya. Priya began to loathe him. She felt empathetic towards Shirin, but not towards Nirmal. If this was how things were, then why did Nirmal marry her in the first place? Why did he drag Shirin into this dark abyss? What was his motive? All these questions clouded her mind.

But since Nirmal had asked Priya to step out, she had no choice but to go. She was intimidated by Nirmal.

Shirin was left alone in her room, alone in her bed, writhing with profound thirst and smouldering from inside.

As soon as Priya and Nirmal left, she closed the door from the inside. She sat on the bed with her legs spread out. Absolutely naked. Primal woman, Shirin Padmavat! Overwhelmed with lust, riddled with desires. However, Shirin didn't desire a man, she craved a woman just like her. She desired herself. Self-love! When there was no one to love you, what else can one do? Priya had also left. Where had Nirmal taken her? Will he do the same thing to Priya that he kept doing to her? Will he strip her naked too? Would he drive her crazy too? Will there be no retribution for her nakedness and madness?

Shirin pressed her breasts with her own hands. She experienced discomfort when pressing them. But women fancied this kind of pain. Women wanted their breastfeeding children to sink their teeth into their breasts. She was supposed to consider herself fortunate.

Shirin gazed at her full thighs. She started caressing herself tenderly. Where did the fingers stop? Why did they stop? She didn't have the strength to bear the fire raging within her own body. The room was locked from the inside. It was enveloped in a silent solitude. How could Shirin divide herself into two halves? The Shirin lying on the bed, and the Shirin who was pressing each part of herself. How was it possible?

Shirin stood on the bed and bent down. She bent further. Her hair fell in front of her. Her breasts grazed her knees.

Shirin placed her hands between her thighs, moaned loudly and fell on the bed. The spring bed started to shudder. Shirin went insane, became unconscious, became a hungry cat. She was moaning fiercely with lust. She wanted to tear her own body apart and devour it.

Blood oozed from her body and yet, Shirin laughed loudly and perspired profusely. She twisted and turned. She writhed. She leaped. Shirin was a starving cat.

Shirin was a fish. She was a dead fish!

Eleven

This was not a triangle. This was not a triangle on whose three vertices Nirmal, Shirin and Priya were placed, either in a stable or unstable manner. Rather, it was a long line. A long and twisted line, whose speed was not determined, nor was its progress decided. People were standing on this line at several places. Exhausted people, defeated people, people fighting for the wrong jihad. People fighting in erroneous ways.

People fight for absurd reasons and in strange circumstances. This fight was terrible. It was fake. People should first fight with themselves. Otherwise, there comes a time when people start taking pleasure in defeating themselves. For defeat becomes their habit, their solitary joy.

Nirmal Padmavat felt happy. He derived pleasure from witnessing Shirin lying like a dead fish on the bed after reaching the peak of sexual pleasure. But the actual defeat was not Shirin's, it was Padmavat's. Shirin was helpless. She had abandoned Mehta. She had closed all doors of emancipation. The fish could not escape from this net. There was no way out of this dark abyss. It was nearly impossible to escape from the dark cave. Shirin Salzberg was in captivity. Ironically, a woman who knew nothing, desired nothing other than physical comfort was confined. She had not fancied any dream, nor love. Shirin Salzburg was terrified of dreams and love. The stories from the New Testament intimidated her. Shirin Salzburg was profoundly aware of the fact that the human self was sinful and guilty by nature. And that is why she kept running away from her emotions and desires. She kept running away from everything but her elder sister's benevolence. She felt calm in her sister's shadow. She felt at peace only after the death of her father. This tranquillity came from sexual gratification.

Both the sisters lived in the same room, slept on the same bed. The mattress is spread on a spring iron cot, and a floral bedsheet covers the mattress.

One fine day, her elder sister explained over a glass of beer that two women could also live together, even enjoy physical intimacy, without having to take favours from men. The elder sister also enlightened her about the process. She kept advancing her moves. Shirin was surprised. She was extremely excited. She surrendered herself completely to her sister. Shirin accepted her advances without any qualms. She did not raise the slightest objection, no refusal at all. No man could have given such profound comfort, such calm arousal, such stimulating physical pain to Shirin. No man could have gifted her that soothing pleasure.

Both sisters used to sleep on the same bed. They locked the doors and windows. The ceiling fan used to run at full speed—even in the months of December and January for at least one to two hours. Shirin was happy that her elder sister is so lovely, and smart! She made her wet. She felt her hands and feet turning cold, and freezing. Yet, she kept clinging to the naked body of her elder sister. She caressed and patted her elder sister with her fingers. Shirin's fingers used to get wet. Her elder sister moaned profusely and bit Shirin's breasts mercilessly. They remained swaddled in happiness, madness, lost in a state of trance.

And in this state, Shirin neither feared religion, nor sin, nor anything else. Her biggest fear was that she would become pregnant, thus she deliberately did not go near any man. Not even when she had the chance. There are those rare occasions when every woman gets trapped at some opportune moment. It becomes difficult to say no. Even if one denies, there is no escape.

Shirin was very young when her mother had shared everything with her. She had told how her father was inadequate in terms of sex. Her mother had told her that all men were beasts. Wild beasts! And women are bound to bow down in front of their savagery. Although they should acquiesce. Even though they should acquiesce, they *should* also despise them, because men are fundamentally ferocious. They only know how to inflict pain on women, they have no idea about how to pleasure her, how to make her happy.

Even then, Shirin loved her father and hovered around him all the time. When her mother helped her change her clothes when going out, she would get enraged. Her father usually gave her a bath, changed her clothes and used to take her out. After returning home, she would eat with her father. She also slept beside her father. Sometimes, her mother would also come to the room to sleep with them. When she awoke, she would see things that she could not decipher. She would get scared. She would go back to sleep in fear. She would often get nightmares. She would see in her dreams various shapes, that a man was morphing into an animal, and that the animal picked up Shirin with his mammoth horns and threw her into a burning fire. There was a humungous mountain. There were many such huge mountains. There were animals over there. Shirin was there on the horns of every animal. She was screaming. She was struggling to set herself free. Her new frock was in tatters and the mountains were shaking. They were on the verge of being shattered. Shirin Salzberg would wake up at this point. She would find her mother sitting on her father's thighs, saying, 'Shirin, are you scared? Make a sign of the cross over your heart and go back to sleep. Don't be afraid.'

The room would be dark. The ceiling fan would be running at full speed. Shirin was still scared. She would wonder whether her mother would kill her father. But Shirin's unconditional love for her father could not last long. Soon, her sister took her father's place. Her mother died. Her father's life underwent a paradigm shift after her mother's untimely demise. He started living a double life. On one side, he would be drowning in wine and on the other, in painting. On one side, death, on the other, religiosity. He continuously created paintings using Christian mythology as the central subject. The paintings weren't selling, nor did he want to sell them. He wanted to die and forget both his daughters.

Both the sisters lived alone in the house. Strangers used to visit and give chocolates and toffees to the elder sister. The younger sister ate the chocolates and would keep smiling. She used to smile and try to decipher what was going on around her, but in vain. The endeavour to understand continues to this day. She wants to understand Nirmal Padmavat. She wants to understand how a robust man like him can be so weak. She wants to seek answers from doctors but is fearful. For she knows Nirmal will kill her if he finds out. But despite being aware of his weakness, she loves him. She admires and reveres him. Nirmal is honest in every moment of his life. He doesn't commit injustices, nor does he ever engage in loose talk. He is intelligent and more diligent than the workers in his mill. He is mightier than the Nepali and Pathan concierges and constables. He is not afraid of anyone or anything. Rather, everyone is intimidated by him. They are apprehensive of what this dark, ugly man will do next.

Nirmal Padmavat visited the share market. The renowned brokers used to follow his suggestions. He used to change the market conditions. The gold prices shot up. Nirmal didn't sell, he made calculations over the telephone and kept buying gold. When Nirmal purchased gold, the prices shot up. Gold and Tata Steel Limited and Punjab National Bank's shares and Hind Motor Company and jute, tea and mica mines—Nirmal dominated the stock exchange. As if he was not a normal human being but a man from Chinese folklore who practised black magic. But suddenly, he stopped visiting the share market. He realized that the market had become a gambling zone and that gambling was beyond his moral compass.

Nirmal Padmavat had both friends as well as enemies in the market. He had an enemy in Vishwajeet Mehta. Mehta was an expert in maintaining enmity. Mehta had instigated a whole bunch of capitalists to stand against Nirmal. This group dominated the newspaper industry. And the newspapers of the capitalists had complete freedom. They could publish anything they wanted to. Now they had their own newspaper company. They had also imported a rotary machine. They had reporters and editors who could cook up false news and disperse misinformation. Any random news could be made up and published. Thus, the face of newspapers had undergone a shift. Now they had become weapons in the fight of the capitalists against the public. The public paid for these newspapers and fell prey to the published news without their knowledge. They fell prey to the sensational stories. Newspapers spread rumours of the Third World War. The newspapers spread social ills. The newspapers spread before us a naked web of sick women, sick games and entertainments, and diseased happiness. Because we are freedom-loving citizens of a free country, we are bound to fall into this trap.

We have the freedom of speech and writing. We have the freedom to print news. We have the freedom to publish newspapers. Ironically, although we do have freedom, we do not have the strength to reap the benefits of that freedom. The strength lies with those who have banks, capital, press, machines, paper, import–export licenses, the power to take the country's gold out and bring foreign gold into the country. They have the power. The common man, on the other hand, has the freedom to remain subjugated under that strength. That's all they have!

Nirmal Padmavat was aware of this and wanted to instigate a rebellion. Shirin also knew this and revered Nirmal for it.

It was because of this profound reverence for Nirmal that she left Mehta, her ex-husband, over a trivial matter. Now, despite Nirmal's weakness, she could not abandon him, for she revered him way too much to even think of leaving him. Not for any other reason but for this profound reverence. This reverence was not mere reverence, it was drenched in empathy. The same empathy that Dr Raghuvansh harboured for Kalyani—the woman who lived the life of a prostitute in a faraway foreign land. Nirmal had narrated the story to Shirin. She knows it all.

Kalyani had fallen sick. Nirmal had sworn to never visit her. Dr Raghuvansh had known Kalyani since childhood. She was an intelligent girl but had got lost in the blinding lights of the cityscape of New York. Eventually, she fell ill, so much so that blisters appeared all over her face. Her entire body had turned blue, and she writhed in excruciating pain. She couldn't get up from her bed. Pus kept oozing out from the blisters.

Dr Raghuvansh did not pity her; rather, he harboured compassion for her. The compassion was not diluted with pity. That is because Doctor was aware that once healed, Kalyani would be back to her normal self—she would again become a fierce and terrifying woman! She would morph back into that same fish, which didn't care about anything but water. Thus, he did not pity her, nor did he despise her. He only had compassion in his heart for her. And that compassion was filled with reverence for her life force.

Shirin Padmavat's compassion was filled with reverence for Nirmal's life force. She could not loathe him for some reason. Nirmal tore her flesh, broke her bones in blind thirst, and yet she could not despise him. She didn't even try to defend herself; instead, she surrendered herself to this wild, hungry animal. She kept enduring the pain. She was compassionate. Even though she was sick, hungry, neurotic, homosexual, yet her heart was filled with compassion.

Shirin was akin to the Greek poetess Sappho, living on the tiny island of Lesbos situated on the Aegean Sea. Sappho used to be surrounded by young girls and used to engage in sexual activities with them. She was in love with Atthis. In fact, she was in love with many girls like Atthis. And yet, she did not loathe her husband Kerkylas. She remained compassionate towards her husband and eventually gave birth to a beautiful girl called Cleis. Shirin too wanted to give birth, but she was helpless because Nirmal was weak. Nirmal was sick. Nirmal was surrounded by complications, helplessness and enemies.

Once, Vishwajeet Mehta telephoned Shirin, and she met him at a restaurant. Nirmal was out of Calcutta that day. But the meeting came to no avail as Mehta Sahab could not make Shirin the heroine of philosopher Russell's story in which Mrs Ellerker, influenced by the devil's magic, forced her husband to commit suicide. Shirin is not the heroine of the story. Shirin is the wife of Nirmal Padmavat. Shirin reveres him.

And Nirmal? He is aware that his illness is not physical but mental. He is the victim of an inferiority complex. There is no way to get rid of this feeling. It was Kalyani who could help him emerge from such morbid emotions, but unfortunately, she is resting in Park Street Cemetery. She cannot emerge from the grave. If someone can emerge, that is Priya. But Priya is not Kalyani. Even Shirin is not Kalyani. Nobody else is Kalyani.

Twelve

*P*riya came out of Shirin's bedroom. She felt petrified. *Why is Nirmal Sahab calling me outside? Has he come to know about my relationship with Shirin? Has Shirin told him? Is there anything else? What is the matter?* Priya was terrified. She was overwhelmed. Unknowingly, she had seen Shirin and Nirmal. She had seen both of them in complete nakedness. Fear. Anxiety. An unknown shudder ran through her. *What will happen now? How will it happen?*

The naked black lady standing on a stool in a corner of Shirin's bedroom—she remains naked. Her eyes are blood-red, lips crimson. Shirin writhes in pain. Priya followed Nirmal, ascended the stairs and came to his cottage. Dhanwantlal was present in the office room. He is an honest private secretary. In his ten years of service, he has taken just two leaves in total. One, on his wedding day, and the other, on the day of his mother's demise. He was initially a typist, but later became the chief clerk in Miller & Miller Co., thereafter, an accountant in the Jute Mill, and now Nirmal's private secretary. The other employees in the office are envious and afraid of him. However, Dhanwantlal deserves friendship, not fear. He is no less than Nirmal Padmavat in terms of honesty and diligence. He never lies, never in front of Nirmal. And thus, at times, he even gets offended with Nirmal about the workings of the company. Why was this firm given the contract to supply raw materials? Why was this man given the job? This auditor is dishonest. This agent asks for a high commission. But every time Dhanwantlal's anger fizzles out on his own. Nirmal is farsighted. He can gauge the future like a seer, which his secretary can't comprehend and is always pleasantly surprised later.

'Sahab, now that the jute mill is shut, how shall we complete the orders? There is a deluge of phone calls. How do we supply them? What to do?' Dhanwantlal was massively furious and devastated.

'Priya, you wait for two minutes, let me deal with this.' Nirmal gave a smile while saying this. Priya felt shy, and wondered how someone could change his temperament in a second! How?

Nirmal received the call, Vishwajeet Mehta was waiting for his final decision on the other end. 'Yes, I am speaking. I accept your proposal. The papers will be ready in an hour. You can sign them when you are ready...Yes, I accept it... Thank you.'

Dhanwantlal felt terrified upon hearing this. His eyes widened with fear. He sat down on the sofa, hanging his head in dismay. Nirmal maintained a subtle smile on his lips. 'I have sold National Jute Mill to Mehta. I bought it for twenty thousand rupees many moons back and am selling it for two lakhs now. Isn't it a fair deal? What do you say, Dhanwant?'

'Please don't do this, Sahab! Do not sell it to Mehta. Padmavat Industries has earned a tremendous foothold in the market. It has earned a great deal of reverence, which will be ruined if you sell it off.'

'Don't worry! The reverence will be intact,' said Nirmal, while scanning through the papers scattered on the table.

'You just think about it, Dhanwant. It's Mehta's respect that would be diminished, not mine. Mehta has bought the National Jute Mill with all its liabilities. The mill's prestige is his prestige now, not mine.'

'But why would you sell it off? If you had visited the mill even once, the workers would have called off the strike. They cannot even raise their heads in your presence.'

Nirmal felt a tinge of dismay at his personal secretary's words. He lifted his eyes and looked at Dr Raghuvansh's daughter. She was sitting cross-legged on one corner of the sofa, skimming through a magazine with her head hanging down. Priya was waiting, albeit intimidated.

Nirmal got up from his chair and stood near the window. He peeked out to see the massive city spreading out as far as his eyes could see. A long procession. Slogans written on placards. Women marched ahead with flags in their hands. People on both sides of the footpath had been watching the procession. Police vehicles followed the procession. Traffic halted at the intersection because of the procession—trams, buses, taxis and trucks. When the procession would cross the intersection, the way for traffic would open. The procession moved slowly, blocking the way for others.

Nirmal watched the procession intently and said, 'The strike would not have ended, Dhanwantlal, even if I went! Workers would have raised their heads, spouted abuses, perhaps they would have thrown stones and bricks. The congregation of workers is like a herd of animals in the jungle. Once they taste blood, they are eternally thirsty for blood. They just need blood, nothing else. Blood in the form of money. Blood, that is, only money! They rebel for a bigger bonus, more wages, more facilities. Lesser working hours. More holidays. Free house to live, free medical treatment, free medicines. The crowd is a bloodthirsty beast. It would continue to suck blood. The crowd does not bother about the source of blood. Vishwajeet Mehta and his friends instigated the crowd at National Jute Mill against me to drag my name through the dirt. He told them the taste of my blood. Now there was no point in retaining the jute mill. Even if the strike was called off, the workers would not have worked diligently; they would have stolen, broken the machines, they come up with new demands every other day. However, irrespective of who owns the mill, they would do the same. Now that they have tasted blood, it doesn't matter to them if the blood is Mehta's or Padmavat's. I had not expected Mehta would buy National Jute Mill. Once again, he has lost the game. He wouldn't be able to run the mill efficiently, Dhanwantlal. He wouldn't be able to complete even one order. His prestige will be jeopardized. His factory would be seized. Just give it a thought to understand my point.'

Nirmal would have continued to speak but Dhanwantlal walked out of the room with a smile. Perhaps he would descend from the lift and visit National Jute Mill straight away. He would speak to the leaders of the workers. The strike must not be called off now, no matter what!

After Dhanwantlal's departure from the room, Priya felt more intimidated. It is written in physiology books that a mentally frustrated person is even more dangerous. They want to forget their physical limitations by inflicting pain on others. They want to take revenge for their shortcomings by making others suffer. *God knows what's in store*, she thought.

She was still flipping through the magazine, her head down. Nirmal continued to watch the scattered city from the window. Padmavat was not thinking about anything, nor had he given a single thought to why he had pulled Priya out of Shirin's room. Was it just to show Shirin his strength? Priya was pondering over this.

Priya thought of standing in Shirin's shoes. There was a different kind of joy in enduring pain. The joy of self-torture. She could easily stand in Shirin's shoes if she intended to. No one can really stop her. She had not only studied medical science books but had also gathered experience. She had seen the world and its workings. If she wanted, she could handle Nirmal Padmavat. She could help Nirmal overcome his limitations, so he doesn't remain weak and vulnerable. Perhaps she could succeed in this endeavour.

Nirmal is a massive mountain of black stones. If she endeavours, greenery can sprout on this mountain. She can trigger a spring of freshwater to flow. Only if she wishes to…

'Why do you persecute Shirin so much, Nirmal Sahab? She is such a fine creature…' Priya began the conversation with this. Nirmal was suddenly taken aback. It was quite unexpected, coming from her.

Nirmal sat beside Priya on the sofa. Gazing into her eyes, he mockingly retorted, 'I am her husband, and I love to annoy her. Why doesn't she protest if she doesn't like it?'

Nirmal looked intently at Priya's curious and tender face, which was gradually turning rigid. Priya did not look at Nirmal. She did not have the courage to look at him. She did not have the strength to read between the lines. There were words camouflaged within words. There were sounds within the words. There were signs within the sounds. She didn't have the strength to decipher whether these cyphers had hidden meanings or not. She had no strength to comprehend the power of zero—the void.

'You speak like old feudal lords.' Priya's face became blank. She had read books written by Sir Walter Scott and Alexandre Dumas—books about British knights and French musketeers. Brave warriors fencing for Madame de la Vallière…Russian princesses…D'Artagnan, known for stealing a precious necklace in return for a kiss on the Queen's tender hands.

'You speak like the old feudal lords, Nirmal Sahab.' Her voice emerged like a hungry snake, breaking out of a closed basket. Spreading her hood, the snake started dancing in the room. Priya herself felt petrified seeing this snake. Shirin had said…Shirin said…Shirin—

'The way I speak is particular to my own style, Priya! It is not borrowed from history books,' Nirmal said in a tender tone and then fell silent. Priya did not have any other questions for him. Even if she did, she was unable to muster the courage to ask him. She had seen the mark of Nirmal's teeth and claws on Shirin's back. Shirin herself had shown the marks on her back and thighs and on different parts of her body. Nirmal morphed into a beast. In the darkness of the night and in the light of the day, he became a beast. Shirin's fair body was filled with dark spots inflicted by him. Peculiar marks. Sick marks. Dark marks.

Shirin Padmavat showed these marks to Priya when they were in the bedroom. Ever since Shirin had met her at the Citizens' Club on the former's birthday, she had been showing these marks to her. They had bonded instantly; Shirin had sought Priya's sympathy and affinity, and thereafter, affection, followed by physical intimacy. She laid on the sofa and moaned while stretching her arms, 'I'm dying, Priya!'

This typical quietus could not be expressed in words, could not be represented in lines. Death was the truth.

And the truth was beyond words, beyond lines. This truth was beyond the limits of time, place and character. This fundamental truth was the untruth.

There was no earth—only the void and the primordial darkness. There was nothingness and a silhouette of two women. There was no man. There was no man. Just a silhouette of two women. There was darkness and nothingness, and no basis for any object. There was no reason, no religion, no form, no condition. Just a silhouette of two women. There were no arms, no hands, no fingers, no knees, no legs, just two fish. Blue fish. And the sea of darkness.

The fish were swimming in the dark, yearning to hold each other. But alas! They did not have arms. They were yearning to cling to each other, but they did not have legs.

The darkness shrank, intensified, and the fish came close. They contracted. They touched. Stuck to each other. Clasped each other. Time stopped. Space evanesced. Identities ended. Two blue fish existed. There was darkness, and there was nought.

One of the fish uttered, 'Come closer, drink me with your lips. Lick my lips with your tongue, brush your body against mine. I'm dying...'

The other fish uttered, 'I'm dying...break my bones! Crush my lips with your teeth. Kill me...for I want to die!'

But it was not easy to die, even if one wanted to die. Thus, the fish remained alive, yearning for death. It is because there was a man alive in their hearts and minds. Just one man—his name was Nirmal Padmavat.

Nirmal Padmavat was eternally present in their lives even while he was away, just like a black bronze statue, ever smiling. The bronze statue was omnipresent in the minds, hearts, in every body part of the two lesbian women.

However, the biggest sorrow for Nirmal was his helpless solitude—the sorrow that had become his companion and sympathizer like an old ailment.

Thirteen

In the 1790s, Marquis de Sade published two novels, *Justine* and *Juliette*. Both books dealt with lesbianism in an extensive manner. They talked about girls living in boarding houses, convents, educational institutions and brothels.

Balzac's novels, *La Fille aux yeux d'or* (*The Girl with the Golden Eyes*), *Le Père Goriot, Séraphîta* and *Scènes de la vie Parisienne*, gave detailed accounts of lesbianism prevalent among the upper-class families in French society.

Alphonse Daudet's book *Sappho*, published in 1884, showed a picturesque life in Paris. Thomas Hardy's novel *Desperate Remedies* was published in 1871.

The protagonist of *Desperate Remedies*, Cytherea, was a girl of eighteen. She had had to engage in a physical relationship with a forty-year-old woman named Miss Aldclyffe. One fine day, Miss Aldclyffe, standing at her bedroom door, asked Cytherea, 'Can I come in, Cytherea?' She advanced towards her, wrapping her in a tight embrace, and said, 'Now kiss me, darling!'

Cytherea refused at first. She felt strange kissing this old and ripe woman. But Aldclyffe had her own logic. She made her 'beloved' understand—'The way I lock my lips with yours, with passion and warmth, why don't you kiss me back in a similar fashion? Why are you so cold? Hasn't any man ever kissed you and made you feel hot and horny? Cytherea, my sweet Cytherea, the amount of love that you bestow upon your lover, I beg you to bestow upon me more love than that! I can assure you that I would give you much more love and contentment than any other man. Love me, Cythe. Please do not bring a stranger between you and me. I cannot endure the pain.'

After fifty-seven years of this novel by Hardy, an Englishwoman and novelist Radclyffe Hall's *The Well of Loneliness* was published in 1928. Stephen Gordon, the protagonist, was a woman belonging to a British upper-class family. She was an only child. She was raised like a man and adorned men's clothes. Also, her name was Stephen, usually a boy's name, and so was her way of life.

In the prime of her youth, Stephen fell in love with her female friend Angela Crossby and compelled her to leave her husband. Eventually, Angela deserted her husband, Ralph Crossby, and began living with Stephen.

Angela loved her beloved Stephen with all her heart. But how could she leave her husband? Angela got both physical gratification and security from her husband. The story of their sordid love was revealed by the turn of events. The neighbourhood came to know that a spinster had been living with a married woman and had been engaging in a physical relationship. This created a ruckus.

Stephen ran away to Paris. The First World War had started. She joined an ambulance unit and started tending to wounded soldiers. She eventually met Mary Llewellyn there. If not Angela, then Llewellyn it is! Stephen engaged in sexual activities with her new lover. After the War ended, both returned to Paris. Thereafter, with the help of

Valérie Seymour, they became a part of a group of lesbian women.

Stephen, Jamie, Llewellyn and Barbara—these four women started gratifying themselves by playing with each other's bodies in the privacy of their closed room. Barbara caught pneumonia and died. Jamie loved Barbara immensely and, unable to endure the pain of her death, committed suicide.

After this twist of fate, Mary Llewellyn started despising her present situation and her individuality. She eloped with a healthy young man, leaving the city. Stephen Gordon is now left all alone! She prays to God:

We have not denied your existence, Almighty.
Thus, you must come and save us. Please accept us.
Give us the right to live in front of the whole world, God!
Kindly acknowledge our existence.

Diana Frederics' memoir was published in 1939. Carol Hales' novel *Wind Woman* was published in the year 1953.

A pianist, Laurel Dean, initially unintentionally, organically, but later intentionally, falls in love with a girl, Zelda, who plays the violin. This love is also 'homosexual'. Laurel felt as if she would die if she didn't caress Zelda's soft and supple body with her fingers. If she couldn't feel the concentric arcs of her body...if she couldn't feel that beautiful and warm flesh...

This is exactly what Priya desires. Priya wants to drown in the depths of Shirin's hot and beautiful flesh. But she is a fish. She doesn't have either hands or feet. Even though she can swim, she cannot drown. But she wants to drown, not in Nirmal, but in Shirin. Because Nirmal is not a human, he is an animal. He is a ferocious wild creature.

The wild animal said, 'I have my own way of speaking. I do not follow someone else's mannerisms. Do not get me wrong, Priya.'

'I did not get you wrong. I know you aren't copying anyone. But Shirin is a fine woman. Why don't you find a reasonable solution? She is your wife after all!

'I had never expected that you would stoop so low! I know exactly what you are referring to. And I do not prefer such innuendos!'

'It is not about your preference, rather it's about the life of a woman. If you cannot give her a child, why do you even go to her in the first place? Why don't you kill her in one go?' Priya rose up from the sofa. She felt an urgent need to walk out of the room. She didn't want to stay there, even for a moment. Nirmal Padmavat was no less than a ruthless, fierce, wild animal!

His mind wanted to taste the wildness of an animal, but not his body. His body began to quiver. Fingers trembled and the trembling fingers reached out for Shirin. Shirin's soft body…mad tide of lust in the body…the tide of the dark ocean…and two fish swimming endlessly…

Suddenly, the entire flat started shaking. The walls were shaking. The Alsatian dogs barked loudly, horribly. It seemed the sky would burst open. It seemed the earth would shatter into pieces.

Kalyani rose in the Park Street Cemetery and made her way to Nirmal Padmavat's flat. She rebuked, 'Why don't you refrain from coming to me when you're aware of your weakness! What for? After all, why?'

'I am not weak. That is exactly what I want you to know, Kalyani!' Nirmal blurted out and closed the door of his flat on the roof of Kalyani Mansion. Now this door will never open. Priya's yelps and yowls do not have the strength to open this door.

Fourteen

Nirmal Padmavat was left with three things—Miller & Miller Co., Kalyani Mansion and West Bengal Bank's shares. The income tax officers were investigating all three accounts.

According to the officers, Nirmal had misappropriated lakhs of income tax money. Apparently, all his registers were fake. The accounts were fraudulent. The budlings he had constructed with years of hard work and brilliance were all a lie.

The officers were of such opinion because Vishwajeet Mehta had confirmed this, Seth Tarachand Manharlal had said so; Khan Bahadur Yusuf Ali, Maharani Shyamgarh, 'Jute Prince' Krishnan Chettiar, Raja Harisingh Dev, everyone was of the same opinion. Vishwajeet Mehta was not alone. If someone was, it was none other than Nirmal Padmavat. He wanted to be left alone. He didn't want to belong to any group of industrialists. Nor did he want to create his own group.

He could have teamed up with Prabhaschandra Niyogi. The old and established capitalists of the city supported him. Their business style was conventional. They didn't invest in new businesses. They converted profits into gold and silver and deposited them in the bank or kept them hidden in the walls of their houses. They lent to banks and other industrialists on special occasions at high interest rates. Loans worth crores of rupees. Interest worth lakhs of rupees. The interest amount multiplied, and proportionally, the number of gold bricks increased. Gradually, the walls thickened. The steel walls covering the gold walls grew thicker. However, the old capitalists did not trust the new businesses. They did not suggest anyone to open new factories. They were eternally mad at the Congress government. They believed that the government was dishonest and was nationalizing all businesses.

On the contrary, the new industrialists did not call the government dishonest. Rather, they considered the government honest and were aware of the fact that honesty could be easily bought. Vishwajeet Mehta was among the new industrialists. The former kings and viceroys had become industrialists now. The former queens had deposited their jewellery and diamonds in the banks. Properties and lands had been sold to start new businesses. Brand new businesses. Massive amounts of gold were smuggled from foreign lands in huge container ships. Maharani Shyamgarh didn't bring them on her own; she had dedicated servants to bring this smuggled gold for her. Gold worth crores of rupees. This gold was deposited in foreign banks. Maharani Sahiba visited foreign lands multiple times a year. New York, London, Paris, Rome. She travelled by her private jet. Vishwajeet Mehta or Seth Tarachand or Krishnan Chettiar accompanied her. Assam tea was sold in the French market. Hazaribagh and Koderma–Tilaiya's mica was purchased in Washington. Foreign machines were purchased and brought to India. New industrial businesses were established in India with the help of foreign industrialists. Rice and wheat harvests dwindled by the day. Production of fashion and luxury items was mushrooming all over. Capitalists always try to outshine the government—they were never a step behind. The private sector would always outperform the public sector. The government would eventually nationalize life insurance companies. Capitalists would invest in transport facilities. The government would work towards the nationalization of the means of transport. Capitalists would invest in modes of entertainment. They would invest in film companies. They would invest in newspaper companies, publishing houses and educational institutions. And the list went on.

The government was honest. Honesty had now become a commodity to be traded. Public votes were being bought. Political parties were being bought. MLAs and MPs could be bought. Ministries could be bought. If one had enough money and wisdom, the entire world could be bought. The new industrialists were aware of this. And that was the reason they had cornered Nirmal Padmavat from all sides. Fierce hunting dogs had been set after him. The net had been cast. The show had commenced.

It was not too late now. Nirmal Padmavat had gauged the situation, it was not too late now.

Prabhaschandra Niyogi had tried to convince him to invite Lakshmichandra Kaviratna and to give him the right to settle all matters. Things would fall into place if he did that. Lakshmichandra would sit in his own car and visit him in his flat at the Great Eastern Hotel. He would open a bottle of whisky and start telephoning everyone, one after another, starting from the income tax commissioner Ramkrishna Goswami; Rambaral Laal, the chief secretary to Seth Tarachand; Sardar Kishan Singh, a special friend of Maharani Shyamgarh; to Prabhat Chakravarty, the leader of Trade Union Congress.

By 11 p.m., everyone would have gathered at Lakshmichandra Kaviratna's flat. This particular flat of the hotel has been taken on rent for days like these. The flat, and a few Anglo-Indian and Bengali girls. The girls would arrive adorning their tight-fitted night dresses, accentuating their curves.

By dawn, Nirmal Padmavat's fate would have been decided. Maharani Shyamgarh would arrive with her gold coins to meet Padmavat. The game of chess would take a crucial turn. The income tax commissioner would have a long and posh car, and there would be a couple of doll-like girls inside the car.

Lakshmichandra Kaviratna is a broker, and he doesn't know anything other than being an incredible middleman. Being a middleman is not a bad job after all, for no work comes to fruition without the engagement of middlemen in our country. There is always someone, of some caste or the other, of some nationality or the other, of some civilization or the other that keeps on engaging in brokerage. Without this, the world cannot move forward. Without this, exchanges won't be possible. Deals cannot happen. Neither of a material thing nor, of any idea.

Niyogi said, 'If you can't do it, I'll telephone Kaviratna. He is a gentleman. He'll come to you himself. At most, you'll have to spend around two lakhs, and probably give some shares in Miller & Miller to Seth Tarachand and enter into a partnership in a new business with Rani Sahiba. You must get ready, Nirmal! This is how the world works today.'

Nirmal Padmavat never followed the methods of others. He answered in one sentence, 'I just want to save Kalyani Mansion.'

Nirmal has an idiosyncratic way of thinking. He recalls incidents from thirty to thirty-five years ago when his mother had eloped with a lorry driver. He yearns for his mother. He wishes for her to come back someday and ask him for a house to live in. For a place to rest. And he would then offer her this Kalyani Mansion. A massive thirty-storied skyscraper!

Nirmal wanted to save this skyscraper for his mother. He doesn't bother about anything else. Neither Dr Raghuvansh, nor Dr Raghuvansh's wife Kalyani, nor Kalyani's daughter Priya…

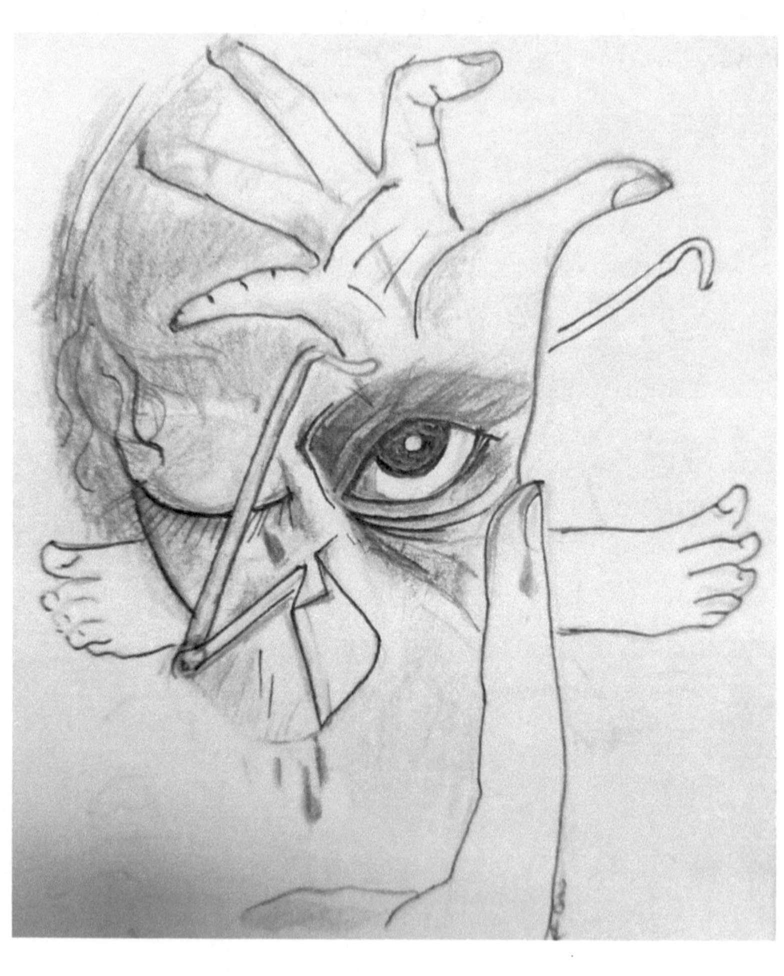

Fifteen

Priya emerges from Nirmal Padmavat's cottage at midnight, just like a ghost emerging from the dark cavern of hell.

This ghost starts descending the stairs of Kalyani Mansion, dragging her fatigued legs. After descending some forty or fifty steps, she fails to carry herself any farther and sits down, taking support of the railing. She is feeling nauseous. Bending forward, she throws up. Her dress gets soiled. Her eyes close. Her intestines start cramping. She feels suffocated because of a putrid smell. She feels breathless.

Priya would die. Although she had come out of hell now, she wouldn't be able to escape. She would die, vomiting like this. Her intestines would gush forth and her liver would rend asunder.

Priya sticks out her tongue to dampen her parched lips. There are remnants of dried vomit on her lips. Eyes are shutting. Nose is burning. Clothes are soaked with alcohol and blood. One of the sleeves of her blouse is ripped open and hanging from her shoulder. One of her breasts peeks out, and there are bloodied marks of nails and teeth there. The front part of the other breast is torn. Her tongue has been bitten.

Priya had protested. But Priya was dead. Priya was dead,

lying face down on the floor of the flat, and Nirmal Padmavat continued drinking rum and kept yelling at the top of his lungs, 'Priya, you have no idea about Nirmal Padmavat's strength!'

Priya was not conscious enough to hear his words. She had fainted. Nirmal Padmavat tried to bring her back to her senses by forcefully inserting a bottle filled with alcohol in her mouth. Every time she would regain consciousness, she would laugh mockingly and blurt out, 'You can do more! I'm still alive. I'm in my senses.' And a moment later she would faint again.

Her sari is tattered in several places. The dark lines of her nerves are visible. Priya regains consciousness. She spreads her legs on the stairs and starts caressing her thighs. Her fingers are swollen. It feeld good to gently caress her thighs. She feels a subtle pain. There is a burning sensation in her lower abdomen, it burns as if flames are rising from there.

Priya presses her stomach with both her hands in a way as if to stop her intestines from bursting out. Pressing her stomach, biting her lower lip with her teeth, eyes closed, she starts descending the stairs. How many more steps she must take? After how many steps could she find some fresh air, openness, some light? Or is it that there is not a single ray of light left in her life?

Priya's legs tremble and she slips. She rolls down the stairs like a bale of cotton.

Nirmal had telephoned the watchman. The lift had been sent upstairs to fetch Priya and had descended already. The liftman and watchman were desperately climbing the stairs in search of Priya. They lifted Priya and did not wait for a moment after that. Priya was laid on the back seat of the car. Within 10 minutes, the car reached Dr Raghuvansh's mansion. The Nepali watchman pressed the doorbell. Dr Raghuvansh was waiting for Priya, although Nirmal had informed him that Priya was at his place and she might be late.

Doctor opened the door. The watchman did not say anything; he took Priya out very carefully from the car, made her lay on the sofa in the drawing room, and quietly left. Dr Raghuvansh felt as if he would go mad, as if he would stop breathing. But he was a doctor, and his sole purpose in life was to save the lives of others. *Is Priya dead? Will she die? Will...* It was 3 a.m. After giving her a bath, Dr Raghuvansh applied medicines to her wounds and carefully laid her on the bed so she could sleep. Sitting on a chair next to her, Dr Raghuvansh was reading a book on gynaecology.

At that very moment, Nirmal Padmavat called him and asked, 'How is Priya's condition now?'

Dr Raghuvansh answered in a calm and steady voice, 'Till a little while ago, she was mumbling in unconsciousness. Now she's asleep. I have given her morphine. She won't wake up before ten or eleven in the morning.'

Doctor hung up the phone after this. He knew that Nirmal would call him. He knew Nirmal would not ask for an apology, nor would he regret his wrongdoings, but he would ask about Priya's health. He knew that someday this would surely happen. He would turn mad. He wouldn't be able to tell apart Priya from Kalyani.

Kalyani had told him about Nirmal Padmavat. She had shared with him the incidents that had unfolded at Shangri-La Hotel. She had shared everything, even the fact that Nirmal was maladjusted in terms of his sexuality. He was sick.

Priya recovered. The wounds on her body healed within a week. Yet she preferred to stay indoors. Shirin telephoned her many times. Some of her friends visited her. Doctor himself told her many times, 'You must meet Nirmal once. He needs you desperately. You'll also feel better after you meet him.'

Priya did not budge. Dr Raghuvansh continued to visit the medical college. He continued with his hospital visits, he continued to see his patients. He continued his regular practice. But one fine night, when Priya had dozed off, he sat down to write a letter to Nirmal Padmavat.

It would seem he had never written a letter to someone before—not even a small one, besides official letters. Maybe he would not write one after this.

There was no need to write this letter. But it's human nature to occasionally do things that may not be needed. Even someone like me falls prey to this kind of move. An old man like me should get at least this much liberty. Anyway...

Perhaps you do not know that I am aware of your old association with Kalyani. You had gifted her a fake diamond necklace. The day she arrived here accompanied by your house helps, she was wearing that necklace. I mocked her when I saw it. Sometimes people act like little children. Why did you put that old and broken necklace around Priya's neck? Do you also have a flair for the dramatics like mediocre men? Melodrama? Did you also want to become the protagonist of that gypsy dance, where the hero marries the daughter of his beloved? Do you think it's possible in real life? Even if it's possible, is it justified?

In any case, I do not wish to burden you with possibilities and questions of propriety. You would not be able to answer any of my questions. In fact, you do not have the answers. The answers rest with me.

I had married Kalyani. And it was certainly not a favour to her. Rather, I had done a favour to myself. I got swamped with studies, then job, and thereafter, my medical profession. So much so that I had no time to marry. When I travelled to the US, by sheer chance and coincidence, I happened to meet Kalyani. She was very sick at that point. On the verge of dying. It was nearly impossible to save her. The disease had spread like poison throughout her system.

But I could save her with the help of my doctor friends. She was beautiful. I had the leisure, so I married her. Much before our marriage, she had disclosed that she had had physical relationships with countless men. That that was her profession. She used to dance in hotels, drank heavily and slept around. I did not despise her for that. I did a favour to myself instead. I married her and brought her back to India. After a while, Priya was born, and unfortunately, within a few years, Kalyani died.

Kalyani had told me that she loved you. Although she had thrown you out of her room, she loved you with all her heart. She was sure of it that you would come back to her. She thought you did not visit her due to some inhibition of yours and not due to the humiliation inflicted on you. She had a strong belief that someday you would let go of your inhibitions and visit her. She thought you would meet another woman who would give you a chance, and gradually your inhibitions would dwindle away. You'll go back to her. She thought you were mightier than me, and thus, you would come over and take her away from me. She had married me just for security. Only because of you, she wanted to be safe, healthy and beautiful. She wanted to secure her life just for you.

I could also understand this. I knew that only a woman like Kalyani could love. Women inclined towards the household could not. Only wayward women could love. Those who did not care about anything. Those who did not follow social norms. Those who were not dictated by morals. Those who did not follow any religion. Such women sold their bodies at every step but did not sell their hearts. Not even as a wife. Not even as a prostitute.

You stood like a massive wall between Kalyani and me while she was alive. I did not know you then. But after burying Kalyani in the cemetery (she had become a Christian after living in New York and was very particular about her religion. Thus, I thought it best to bury her), I was drinking alcohol, and that's when I met you for the first time. I could recognize you the moment I saw you. Kalyani could not have loved a lesser man.

I have also loved you. Kalyani was not around, and you desperately needed love. The mad animal in you needed to be domesticated. I thought Priya would tame you wisely. But you married Shirin Mehta after being trapped in business deals. I felt sad that day for the first time. I felt sad for you.

Shirin Mehta is a homosexual. Many upper-class women used to run after her. Vishwajeet Mehta had brought Shirin to me many times as he wanted to fix Shirin's sexual orientation. I had no remedy for her. I had even referred her to different doctors specializing in that area. But Shirin refused to see any doctor. She loves her life. She loves women.

You married none other than her. Thus, I was hurt. For I knew she wouldn't be able to heal your weakness. Nor could she give you conjugal pleasure. She didn't make you happy, and you remained a beast. You couldn't be a normal human being.

There is no greater happiness than being a normal human being, Nirmal.

If Kalyani was still with us, and you were with her, you would have experienced this.

It is not more difficult to be abnormal than to be extraordinary. One can temporarily become extraordinary by drinking a bottle of alcohol. The intoxication of wealth, a little excess of sexual desires, a little antisocial and immoral activities make a man abnormal. But it is mighty difficult to be ordinary. It is punishing to keep our lifestyle bound to simplicity and mediocrity. Movement is easy, but inertia is difficult.

I wanted you to be extraordinary in your achievements, not in your circumstances. I wanted you to be exceptional in knowledge, strength, courage, patience, and in your soul, not in your physicality. However, all this was not possible while being in a relationship with Shirin, because...

The journey of a man began with his family. First of all, the milieu and situation of the family impacted his personality and the work he undertook. Shirin's influence made the animal in you wilder.

And Kalyani's daughter Priya fell prey to this wildness of yours.

However, even as a prey, Priya had the courage to do what Kalyani had intended. You have become a man. The weakness you were experiencing, it magically vanished. I saw Priya's body soaked in blood. You raped her. Not once, but many times. The power that Kalyani had snatched away from you; Priya returned it back. That's a welcome change.

I am not at all sad that you treated my daughter like a monster. I am rather happy because Priya too became a homosexual after befriending Shirin. And only such kind of monstrous behaviour could make her a normal, straight woman again. Now she is not sick anymore. Rather, she has become healthy. She has finally become normal, straight.

You are surrounded by troubles from all sides. Your life is in jeopardy. Most of the people in the city are against you. You are being slandered in newspapers. But I am not worried about these happenings. If your mind remains calm, no one can defeat you. You will remain at the top. Just keep your mind in your control.

This letter has turned into a long sermon. This should not have happened. There was no need to preach to you. Do not pay attention to this unnecessary sermon of mine. I have grown quite old now.

Whatever money and property I have gathered so far, I will donate them to the neurological department of Sheetaldas Medical College. Now I do not possess anything.

There is nothing left for which the world might need me, and vice versa.

I desperately need sleep, and what could be more tranquillizing than death!'

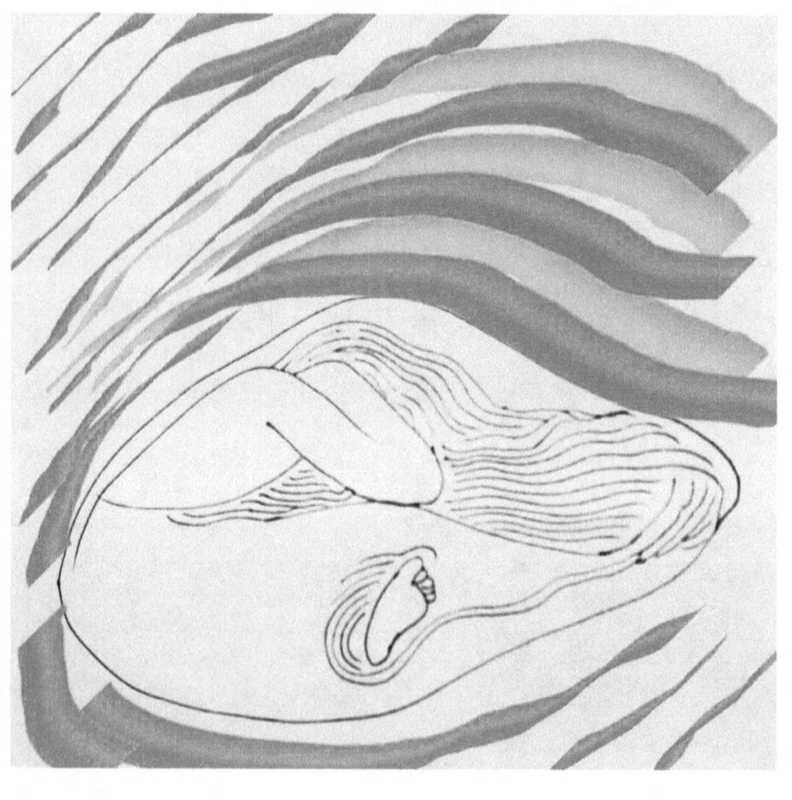

Sixteen

After sealing the letter for Nirmal Padmavat in an envelope, Dr Raghuvansh picked a bottle of brandy from the almirah. Filling his glass, he kept drinking for a long time. Then he fell asleep on the table with his arms stretched out.

Priya woke up in the morning to the shouts of the servants and the ruckus created by people. She had slept with the door locked from inside. Oblivious. Unaware.

When she reached her father's room, the death certificate was being drafted. Dr Raghuvansh had died of a brain haemorrhage. His wound was festering inside. Overdrinking made it burst.

The dead body had been covered with a white shroud. Priya walked towards the body, having covered her head with her dupatta. Removing the white shroud from his face, she looked at her father for the last time and came near his feet to pay obeisance. The moment she turned back towards her room, she felt dizzy. She was about to lose her balance and fall when Nirmal, who was standing behind her, came to her aid. Priya gathered herself and said, 'I just felt a bit dizzy. I'm fine now,' and went to a corner to stand.

The dead body remained there for a few hours. The bier was being prepared outside. Many doctors, medical college students and nurses kept pouring in. Old friends, ex-patients, relatives, everybody kept coming. Priya remained standing quietly in the corner—solemn, indifferent, as if her father had not passed away. As if all this was a drama. A tragic drama.

The drama would be over and Dr Raghuvansh would rise from his slumber and say, 'Priya, so many people have gathered here, see if you can arrange some coffee for the guests…'

The dead body, covered with a silk sheet and flowers, lay in front of her. But it was hard to believe. It is not easy to experience death.

This was the second time Priya had experienced death. She had seen her mother's death in the hospital, among nurses and doctors. Bottles of medicines. Aspirator. Rubber tubes. Operation theatre. The 1,000-watt bulb blazing overhead. Priya remembered the nurse who had taken her out. Near the flower beds in a park. Priya had said, 'Nurse, pluck me the big flower from there, I want to give it to my mother. She loves flowers.'

She wanted to give a sunflower to her father too. A flower none other than the sunflower—Priya!

The bier was placed on a big truck. The funeral procession left for the crematorium. Priya kept sitting near Dr Raghuvansh's feet. She kept gazing at Nirmal Padmavat who was walking bare feet behind the truck. He was wearing a Shantipuri dhoti and had draped a white shawl over his white vest. Nirmal was walking amidst a crowd of thousands of people and yet he stood out, for he was above them. He was alone. As if Dr Raghuvansh's dead body was with him. As if he was carrying the dead body on his high and strong shoulders like a giant monster. He was walking alone towards the red, burning cremation ground on the horizon…all alone. Dr Raghuvansh's dead body. Kalyani's dead body. Priya and Shirin's dead body. Nirmal isn't carrying the weight of just one dead body on his shoulders,

Priya then closed her eyes and silently saluted Nirmal.

Upon unloading Dr Raghuvansh's body from the truck, it was taken to the electric crematorium of Keoratola. Priya kept standing outside. Thousands of people thronged outside. Priya was searching desperately for Nirmal in the crowd. Nirmal was nowhere to be seen. Dr Raghuvansh's body was burning. Nirmal was nowhere to be seen.

Priya returned home after the rituals in a hand-pulled rickshaw. She was whimpering with anger and pain. She stayed in bed all day, listening to the radio and reading letters and telegrams filled with empathy and compassion. She was engrossed in reading the obituaries published in different newspapers. She patiently heard the tearful voices of her father's friends, well-wishers, disciples and associates on the telephone. Meanwhile, she kept waiting. For whom? Ironically, Nirmal didn't even telephone her, nor did Shirin visit her.

The entire week flew by. Priya was swamped in handing over her father's laboratory and library to the workers of Sheetaldas Medical College. He had donated all his movable and immovable properties to the College. He had left nothing for Priya. Nothing. Even the house they inhabited was a rented one. Where will she go now?

After eight days of Dr Raghuvansh's passing, Priya came out of her house and boarded a taxi. She had an envelope that carried Dr Raghuvansh's letter for Nirmal. Priya had not read the letter.

Priya reached Nirmal's flat. The Alsatian dogs started barking at the gate. Nirmal said, 'Come inside, Priya.'

The room was a mess like the other day, and nothing

had been moved. The vase on the floor was broken, cigarette buds and books were scattered, and the mattress of the sofa was torn. The table was also not in its place. Empty liquor bottles. Glass. Even the glass ewer was lying to one side.

There was the same stench emanating from the room that had been following Priya since the night her father had died. The stench that was making Priya unconscious. That same strong stench.

Priya came inside and kept the envelope on the table. Nirmal rose from the sofa and gazed straight into Priya's eyes, just like a hunter Bull Terrier gazes sharply towards a herd of deer. He was sad, serious, angry, worn out and extremely tired. Priya took two steps back. She stood holding on to the curtain hanging from the lintel of the door. Nirmal stubbed out the cigarette butt in the ashtray and advanced towards Priya in haste. A subtle smile played on Priya's lips. An amalgam of peace, sweetness, compassion, poison, sunflowers and smiles!

She clung to the curtain hanging from the lintel of the door. But Nirmal did not advance further, rather retreated. He quietly went and sat on the nearby armchair. He was exhausted from deep within. Priya came closer without saying a word. She sat on the corner of the sofa, very quietly.

Time passed by in a jiffy. Both sat there, without speaking a word, just like strangers, for almost half an hour. Puncturing the silence, Priya asked, 'Where are the keys to the almirah? I want to make coffee! Would you like to have some coffee?'

'The almirah is open. While you prepare the coffee, I'll go down to the office. Income tax officers are waiting for me. Miller & Miller's audit is going on.'

A couple of income tax officers were sitting in his office. They were investigating the accounts of the company. His secretary, Dhanwantlal; Shrinivas Sarvadhikari, the income tax commissioner; Ramachandran, the manager of Miller & Miller Co.; a couple of clerical staff; and Lakshmichandra Kaviratna. Despite Nirmal's refusal, Prabhaschandra Niyogi had sent Kaviratna to help him.

Nirmal Padmavat did not stop there. Everyone was gazing at him with inquisitive eyes, but he went straight to his chamber. Shrinivas Sarvadhikari and Lakshmichandra joined him after some time. Lakshmichandra said with a smile, 'Accounts have been audited and they could not find any faults. You must not worry at all, Padmavat ji. Everything has been sorted out. I have already spoken with Dhanwantlal. The matter has also been discussed and decided upon with the Commissioner.'

'What has been decided upon?' Nirmal sat straight. 'Nobody has the right to decide anything about Miller & Miller. Kaviratna ji, please ask the Commissioner to tell me clearly, whatever it is that he has to say.'

There was fear and greed in Shrinivas Sarvadhikari's eyes. He was a robust man. Midlife paunch, tiny eyes. Previously he had been a professor of economics in a college. He became an income tax officer after passing the Service Commission exam, and now he is a commissioner. He had never taken a bribe in his life. He was about to retire in a couple of years. Still, he never took a bribe. He was scared before and was scared even now. Retirement was just around the corner and yet he could not build a house of his own. He doesn't even own a car. His shoulders were heavy with the responsibility of his youngest daughter's marriage; he wanted to get her married by the year-end. Unfortunately, all potential grooms demanded a dowry no less than the huge expenses of going abroad. They even demanded a car. The girl was not conventionally beautiful. On top of that, she had consulted a gynaecologist around two to three times at her tender age, which was looked down upon. His wife would say, 'Everyone takes bribes. Why don't you? Sinha Sahib has built a superb mansion in Ranchi. All three sons of Chopra Sahab are studying in London. Shastri is your junior, and yet his wife visits Kashmir every year during summer.'

Sarvadhikari is an honest man. 'The fundamental issue is that Mr Padmavat's Miller & Miller Co. has shown wrong income tax returns since the last four years,' Kaviratna said. 'According to the government audit reports, a total sum of thirty lakhs have been misappropriated.

'But this misappropriation can be rectified. Sarvadhikari Sahab has demanded just fifty thousand rupees, nothing more. I have spoken with him. The misappropriation of thirty lakhs would disappear if we paid fifty thousand. Ask Dhanwantlal to arrange for cash payment. Niyogi ji said that if you have difficulty paying the sum in cash, he could arrange it for you,' Kaviratna said all this with a subtle smile on his face.

Nirmal Padmavat was lost in his own thoughts. He was thinking about neither the fifty thousand nor Miller & Miller, rather, he was thinking about his tea shop in Karachi that was dismantled by the police. Today Miller & Miller is about to be dismantled. Tomorrow it might be Kalyani Mansion…

Nirmal started laughing. Kalyani Mansion might be taken away from him tomorrow. Either tomorrow or the day after or on the fourth day. Then he said in a stern voice, 'I have never done anything dishonest in my life. I will not offer even a penny in bribe…all of you can leave. Everyone, just go away. I will not tell anyone that income tax officers had asked for a bribe. I won't say anything, I will not complain, or else I could have informed the police. I could have requested

CID officers to sit in the next room. I could have recorded your conversations on a tape recorder. I could have done all of these, but I didn't. You can leave. I'll not pay any bribe.'

'You can give it a second thought, Nirmal Sahab.' There was sympathy in Kaviratna's tone. 'You'll not get a chance like this again. I do not stand to gain anything from this. I won't get even a hundred rupees in this deal, and yet I have convinced Sarvadhikari ji in your favour. Please give it a second thought.'

Nirmal Padmavat quietly listened to Kaviratna and Sarvadhikari for a very long time. National Jute Mill has shut down; Vishwajeet Mehta does not have the spine to restart the mill. The government is about to shut down Miller & Miller. All business interests of Padmavat Industries have been affected. Soon, Kalyani Mansion would also be taken away. Either tomorrow or the day after or on the fourth day. And there is only one way to escape all of this, that is, a sum of fifty thousand rupees.

'Are you able to comprehend the entire situation, Padmavat ji?' Lakshmichandra Kaviratna asked.

'Yes,' replied Padmavat, hanging his head. He gazed at his hands on the table. These hands were his own.

'Then what have you finally decided?' Sarvadhikari's eyes were still sparkling with greed. Nirmal Padmavat clenched both his hands into fists. Fish had started to swell on his biceps. He stood up and said, 'No, I will not pay a bribe.'

This is sheer madness. It's nothing less than a suicide. No wise man would do this in today's day and time. No sensible person would do this. But Nirmal Padmavat was not a sensible person. He was insane, a savage! Nirmal took the lift back to his floor, and on reaching his flat, asked, 'So Priya, I hope the coffee has not gone cold?'

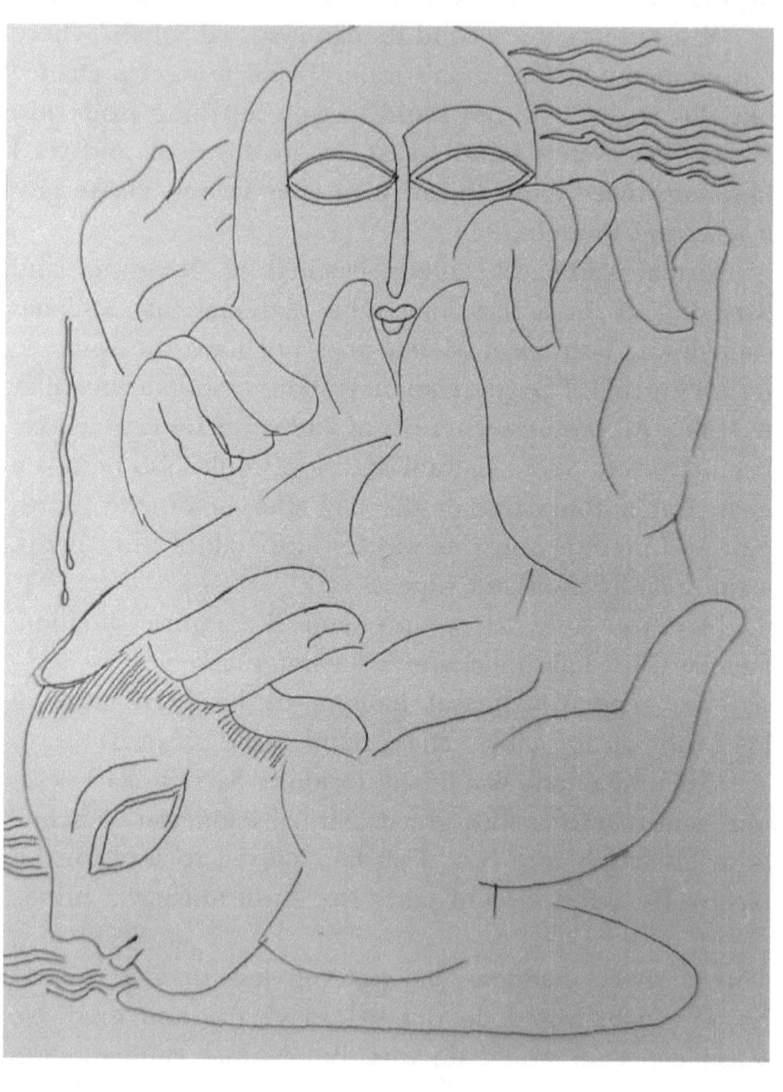

Seventeen

There was no meaning left in Shirin Padmavat's life. Most of the time she stayed in her room, devouring glasses of vermouth, sherry, port, rum. Rotberger's red wine. Yellow cognac. White Bordeaux in a frosted glass. Chianti. Gin in the afternoon. Armagnac in the evening. The intoxication of a lonely night and Burgundy. Intoxication of any alcohol. Intoxication of thoughts. The intoxication of love and forgetfulness too...

She kept deceiving herself. She kept lying down, as if inflicted with paralysis. Her female friends visited her often. Society ladies! The rich women came to meet her. They engaged in loose talk and laughed for a while, and dispersed. However, Priya didn't turn up. Not even for a moment.

Shirin knew that Priya was in Nirmal's flat. She must be making coffee. Or humming a song. Sleeping. Roaming on the terrace. She must be smiling, wearing a veil of coyness. Shirin knew all this and the very thoughts drowned her further in a pool of alcohol. Her throat burned, chest burned, and so did her soul.

Nirmal Padmavat had not forgotten Shirin. He knew that Shirin was in her bedroom. With a woman. All alone. And he knows she must be waiting for him. Waiting for him or for Priya? But he never went to her bedroom, nor did he ever send Priya. He wanted Shirin to come upstairs to his flat. And he feels that if she cannot come, she should leave Kalyani Mansion for good, and should go someplace, anyplace. If she doesn't find a place to go to, she could go back to Vishwajeet Mehta. Mehta would accept Shirin. Mehta would accept anything that belongs to Nirmal.

However, Nirmal was awaiting Shirin's final decision. *What will she do?*

Shirin was desperately waiting for Priya's decision. *What will she do?* Shirin yearns to know what's cooking in Priya's mind.

Miller & Miller Co. was gone, and gone was Dhanwantlal. Nirmal had dismissed his private secretary because he had overheard Dhanwantlal's conversation with Lakshmichandra Kaviratna. The former had said that he would see how far Nirmal Padmavat could go this way. Dhanwantlal had failed to understand Nirmal, and Nirmal loathed people who misinterpreted his actions.

Dhanwantlal was gone. Many other things were gone. But what about Kalyani Mansion?

Nirmal Padmavat had chosen the path of dishonesty for the first time in his life. For the first time, he had misappropriated his accounts. He paid the income tax and penalty amount with the money received from the sale of National Jute Mill and the shares of West Bengal Bank. It was a massive sum of around thirty-five lakh rupees. And then he showed that he had had to take a few lakhs as a loan from Dr Raghuvansh while constructing Kalyani Mansion. He proved that the money did not belong to Dr Raghuvansh. That it belonged to Kalyani, and that she had left the money with her husband before she died—it was in the form of jewellery and precious gems, not cash.

And that, to repay the debt, Nirmal Padmavat had to sell off Kalyani Mansion to Priya. This was the only way to save Kalyani Mansion from being confiscated. Otherwise, this thirty-storey mansion would have been seized or auctioned away. Perhaps it would have been purchased by Vishwajeet Mehta, Maharani Shyamgarh or Seth Tarachand.

Nirmal handed over the documents to Priya. He took her to the Registrar, and in no time, the papers were signed. Priya had no qualms about it; she had no objections. She understood that all these were just legalities and that Nirmal did not have any ulterior motives. She knew that he wanted to safeguard Kalyani's memory. He wanted to keep the memories of her mother with him.

Padmavat Industries went bankrupt. Nirmal Padmavat was broke. He was left with nothing except a big sapphire on a finger of his right hand. Nothing else. Nothing nowhere.

Escorting Priya to the lift, he said, 'You go upstairs. I'll come in a while.'

Nirmal crossed the road to the other side and stood there. There was a small pond beside the road. There are trees and plants and concrete benches all around the pond. The pond is old. Peculiar bushes had grown on the marble jetty. Unusual flowers gazed at their own smiles reflected on the blue water's clear surface. On the last step of the jetty, there was an Anglo-Indian girl sitting quietly. She was looking at the bushes growing in the water, lost in her thoughts.

Kalyani Mansion's shadow spread over the surface of the still waters of the pond. Nirmal was standing on the jetty, gazing at the shimmering shadow. White shadow on the blue waters!

All of a sudden, a big fish leapt up, piercing the surface of the water. Kalyani Mansion began to shake. It trembled for a long time…Nirmal Padmavat kept looking at it, lost and amazed. He is visiting the pond for the first time and it is the first time he is seeing Kalyani Mansion fade away.

Nirmal turned his face towards his house. The highest tower in the city—Kalyani Mansion! As tall as Nirmal, trembling and quivering on the surface of the water.

Another fish leapt up.

The Anglo-Indian girl sitting on the last step recognized Nirmal and was filled with amazement.

Mr Padmavat is standing here? Alone? she thought and advanced towards him. She folded her hands to pay obeisance.

Nirmal smiled. 'How are you doing, Miss? Where are you working?'

'Everything is fine, Sir! I'm getting married next week. Hope you'll come for the wedding?' She asked him and gave a smile. Just like a freshly bloomed flower. Just like beauty, just like love!

It dawns on Nirmal that he is also married. He is married to Shirin Padmavat. But he has never looked at Shirin like a normal woman. Never looked at her like a woman. He has merely considered her as one of the floors of Kalyani Mansion, or as a flat where he can spend a night. An insignificant part of the power loom at National Jute Mill. Any one of the ledgers of Miller & Miller.

Nirmal Padmavat had never considered or accepted Shirin Padmavat the way he should have. It wasn't just about her—he had not seen any human being around him through that lens, nor did he ever see society in a different light. He had never tried to decipher the workings of the society he inhabited. Perhaps he never got the time or chance to do so. Today he has the time after so many years. It is because he is back on the footpath once again. He has become a proletarian again; he has had an old association with footpaths. Karachi's footpath, Bombay's footpath, New

York, Washington, Cairo, Calcutta's footpath. He knew them all. There is no difference in footpaths of different places, for footpaths in all cities are the same. The only difference is in the houses, and in the people inhabiting them. There is a difference in the way people live their lives, in their culture, in their history.

Nirmal had never tried to understand this difference, and perhaps that is the reason why he was brought to the footpath once again. He could not win against Vishwajeet Mehta and his friends. It is because he was unaware of the workings of this city. He did not approve of the law of this city! The law defeated him brutally. Nirmal's own steel defeated him…

That girl left after greeting him. She is getting married next week. Nirmal comes out from the edge of the pond. A footpath along the road. Cars and taxis are running on the road, but the footpath is empty. Nobody walks on foot on Princess Street.

Nirmal crosses the road—on foot. He reaches the lift of Kalyani Mansion. The liftman is new and he does not recognize Nirmal. He asks, 'Where do you want to go?'

'Thirtieth floor,' Nirmal says, and goes ahead and stands in front of the mirror in the lift. A couple of people enter the lift. There is a plump Punjabi woman, Mrs Singh. Two men are conversing about racehorses. Another one has his nose in a book. The lift starts going up. Mrs Singh recognizes Nirmal. She gives a smile and bows her head in reverence. While managing two bags of wheat in each of her hands, she says, 'Namaste, Padmavat Sahab. I've heard that you've sold this mansion? To a daughter of some doctor… Is it true?'

'Yes, I have sold it off,' Nirmal answers laughingly. The rows of his white teeth sparkle. The men in the lift are startled. The liftman shudders. He realizes that he is with the owner of Kalyani Mansion—Nirmal Padmavat.

One by one, everyone gets out. Nirmal is the last one left on the lift. The liftman, filled with fear and embarrassment, bows his head and says, 'I could not recognize Sahab. Please forgive me.'

'There is no need to recognize me. The owner of this building lives upstairs. Try to recognize her; that would be enough.' Saying these words, he gets off the lift at Shirin's floor.

Nirmal had not met Shirin for more than three weeks. She lay in bed, unconscious in sleep, intoxicated with liquor. In these three weeks she has done nothing except drink and create a ruckus with high society's cheap women. Whenever she would miss Nirmal, she would drink to her gills to deal with her loneliness. She would often go mad and scratch her own flesh in desperation. Her own flesh...

Shirin opened her eyes but did not rise from the bed. She stretched and smiled. There was a searing pain in her smile. She had been desperately waiting for Nirmal.

Perhaps, for the first time, Nirmal realized that there was pain in that smile. And *that* lone smile was the answer to all questions, the cure for every pain, the strength to endure every predicament. This smile didn't have anything else camouflaged in it. It was a woman smiling, gazing at her man. The smile was pregnant with pain, pride, complaints and grievances, and dedication...

He advanced towards the bed and plopped himself down near Shirin's head. When he began to entwine his fingers in her scattered locks, she said, 'Take me out of this city, Nirmal. I'll die here.'

Nirmal smiled. Placing her head on his lap, he said, 'I'll take you wherever you want to go...I'll take you with me. But for now, don't say anything else. Do not ask any questions.'

Shirin didn't even have any questions. All the questions in her mind had died in the last three weeks. She herself had died.

When did they both fall asleep, neither could realize. She fell asleep with her head on her husband's left arm. She was the first to wake up in the morning. Nirmal kept sleeping. She went to the bathroom. Kept bathing for a long time. Kept floating, occasionally submerging herself, in the big bathtub filled with water. Kept sprinkling water on her face, humming an old song...

> It rained. Water flooded the dried-up river,
> water flooded...
> The dead blue fish
> came back to life.
> Soul full of love, love full of thirst...
> The river flooded with water
> for the blue fish
> that had died of thirst.
> It rained!

Nirmal Padmavat woke up. Still, his eyes remained shut and he kept listening to the strange song in an unknown language and he felt it was raining outside. The dried-up river had now been flooded with water. The tide had started rising in the sea... The tide of life...Shirin opened the door and entered the room. She had tied her black hair into a Manipuri bun! There was a thick line—appearing like blood—in the middle parting of her hair—*sindoor*. The thick line of sindoor was glowing on her head and Shirin Padmavat's entire face had become colourful. There was coyness in this colour. There was pride. And there was compassion!

As if by magic, as if some compulsion in her existence had brought Shirin very close to Nirmal for the first time! Like a bride switching off the light in her bedroom on the first night.

Nirmal Padmavat silently got down from the bed and stood smiling. He didn't have anything to say to Shirin, no words, no language in which to speak. They stood before each other and had no words, no language.

The river had dried up. The sea had dried up. That fish jumping on the blue waves was dead. And from the body of the dead fish a woman was emerging; rising up:

Shirin Padmavat!

Shirin had been born. Now she won't die. Love dies. Lust dies. Not compassion. Only compassion never dies.

Glossary

Aadi Yug	Beginning of the Vedic/new era
Abhayamudra	A symbolic gesture of fearlessness—representing protection, peace, benevolence and the dispelling of fear—in Hinduism and Buddhism
Beat Generation	A literary subculture movement started by a group of authors whose work explored and influenced American culture and politics in the post-World War II era. Notable writers include: William S. Burroughs, Allen Ginsberg and Jack Kerouac
Been	Or pungi, is a Hindu folk music reed pipe instrument made from a dry hollowed gourd with two bamboo attachments
Bela	Jasmine flowers
Halla gadi	Unremarkable black vans ferrying lathi-wielding men who drive terror through the hearts of hawkers and keep them on tenterhooks
Hungry Generation	A literary movement in the Bengali

	language launched by what is known today as the Hungryalist quartet, i.e., Shakti Chattopadhyay, Malay Roy Choudhury, Samir Roychoudhury and Debi Roy (alias Haradhon Dhara), during the 1960s in Kolkata, India
Jihad	The spiritual struggle within oneself against sin
Kaleji	Or mutton liver, is a highly flavourful and nutrient-rich dish often made during special occasions
Khadaga	A crescent-shaped sword or a giant sickle
Khansama	A male cook, who often also manages domestic matters in a large household
Lalbibi	Lower-class sex workers
Moksha	A term in Jainism, Buddhism, Hinduism and Sikhism for various forms of emancipation, liberation, nirvana or release. In Hindu traditions, moksha is a central concept and the utmost aim of human life; the other three aims are dharma (virtuous, proper, moral life); artha (material prosperity, income security, means of life); and kama (pleasure, sensuality, emotional fulfillment)
Sindoor	A traditional vermillion red or orange-red or maroon cosmetic powder from South Asia, usually worn by married women along the part of their hairline

Tandoori	A cooking method that involves marinating meat, typically chicken, in yogurt and spices, and then cooking it in a tandoor, a cylindrical clay oven
Teleprinter	Once considered cutting-edge technology in news transmission
Varadamudra	A symbolic gesture of generosity—signifying offering, welcome, charity, giving, compassion and sincerity—in Hinduism and Buddhism
Zamindar	An autonomous or semi-autonomous feudal lord of a zamindari or feudal estate in pre-Independence India